EVERY TIME WE FALL IN LOVE

New York Sullivans

Bella Andre

EVERY TIME WE FALL IN LOVE

New York Sullivans

© 2018 Bella Andre

Sign up for Bella's New Release Newsletter

www.BellaAndre.com/newsletter

bella@bellaandre.com

www.BellaAndre.com

Bella on Twitter: @bellaandre

Bella on Facebook: facebook.com/bellaandrefans

Harry Sullivan has always put his family first, even when it meant losing Molly—his one true love. He's never been able to forget her, even after fifteen years. Now that his siblings are all blissfully happy, Harry hopes it's not too late for his own happily-ever-after. But then his doorbell rings...and one look at the teenage girl standing on his doorstep changes absolutely everything.

Molly never thought she'd see Harry Sullivan again, so she's beyond stunned when her fifteen-year-old daughter brings him back into her life. At eighteen, Harry was already strong, sexy and honorable. And now that he's even more handsome, more brilliant, more loyal and caring? Molly can't stop herself from falling in love with him all over again. Especially when his kisses and the sizzling attraction between them are hotter than ever.

But with more at stake now than they ever thought possible, will they be able to move beyond the mistakes they both made in the past and fall in love forever this time?

A note from Bella

For the past two years, I have been waiting impatiently to write Harry Sullivan's story. After all, who wouldn't fall for a brilliant hero who has never forgotten his first love, cares deeply about his family…and looks seriously sexy in glasses?

Compared to his three siblings, Harry has always looked like he has it all together. Which is why it shocks everyone, including him, when he's the New York Sullivan whose life is in the biggest upheaval.

I hope you absolutely love Harry and Molly's second-chance romance. They've both certainly waited long enough for it!

Happy reading,
Bella Andre

P.S. Watch for Cassie Sullivan's story, the first of seven Maine Sullivans, coming soon!

P.P.S. Please be sure to sign up for my newsletter (bellaandre.com/newsletter) so you don't miss out on any new book release announcements.

CHAPTER ONE

It was the perfect double engagement party for Harry Sullivan's brother, Drake, and his fiancée, Rosa—and Harry's sister, Suzanne, and her fiancé, Roman. The adults were all happily chatting. The kids were running around laughing and playing. Harry's dog, Aldwin, was keeping a careful watch on everyone's plates in hopes that food would fall.

And all the while, Harry couldn't stop thinking about Molly Connal.

They'd met as freshmen at Columbia University, and he'd immediately fallen head over heels for her. Not only because of her beauty, but also because her brain constantly astounded him. He couldn't believe his luck when she'd felt the same way about him.

Molly had been the one constant bright light in his life—she was fun, brilliant, and sinfully sexy. Where life with his family had been a continual roller coaster, Molly had always been both gentle and easygoing. So much so that he'd taken her completely for granted, putting her last time and time again.

It didn't help that Harry's family had been going through one of its roughest spells the year he and Molly were dating. Harry and his siblings—Alec was the oldest, with Harry next, then Suzanne and Drake— were a very tight-knit group. The death of their mother when Drake was just a toddler had only brought them closer, especially when their father all but disappeared from their lives in his grief.

During Harry's freshman year in college, Drake and Suzanne had been in high school and needed his guidance on everything from schoolwork to college applications. Alec had needed a sober wingman to keep him from getting into trouble at the bars he'd gone to far too often. But it was their father, still adrift in grief over losing their mother and his wife, who had needed Harry's help most of all.

He would never forget the night he'd found his dad passed out on the floor of his lake house, his clothes unchanged for days, food- and sleep-deprived and reeking from too much booze. It had not only been the anniversary of Harry's mother's death—it had also been Molly's birthday.

That night, Harry had known he had to set Molly free, even though it felt like cutting out the brightest, sweetest, warmest part of his heart. But she deserved better than a boyfriend who was rarely able to be there for her, even if he'd always done his best to make things up to her when he was around. After ending things with her, he'd made sure to stay away, no matter how tempted he'd been over the years to find her, to ask for a second chance.

But now—at long last—his family was in a good place. Alec was happily married and had recently transitioned from airplane mogul to chef at his wife Cordelia's garden center. Suzanne had found love with her former bodyguard, Roman. Drake and Rosa had found love in the most unlikely of circumstances as well. And best of all, though their father had struggled for three decades with the loss of their mother, it now seemed that William was ready to fully live his life— and to be a real father again.

With Harry's siblings' personal and professional lives settled, he felt as though he could finally take a deep breath. And a clear-eyed look at his *own* life.

Since graduating with a PhD in medieval history, he'd poured his passion into teaching, research, and writing as a professor at Columbia University. On the other side of the spectrum, jousting gave him a physical outlet to turn to when burying himself in books didn't cut it. And he hadn't been a monk, of course.

But he'd never fallen in love again.

No other woman had ever come close to being as smart, as fun, or as sexy as Molly. Their connection had been so natural, so passionate, so damned good.

And he'd never stopped missing her.

After they'd broken up at the end of freshman year, Molly hadn't returned to Columbia. Countless times, Harry had wanted to search for her, to ask her to come back and be with him again. But he'd never allowed himself to do it, not while the issues in his family hadn't gone away.

Only, now that things *had* changed, what if he finally looked her up? What if he showed up on her doorstep out of the blue and told her that his biggest regret was breaking her heart? What if he asked her to give him a second chance?

Would she invite him inside and hear him out?

Or was she already married with a great husband and cute kids, having moved on with her life, even though he hadn't?

Aldwin got up slowly and walked over to put his broad head beneath Harry's hand while making a low, rumbly sound—the dog's way of saying he needed to go outside to take care of business.

Harry had adopted Aldwin after seeing him on one of the animal-shelter buses that came to the nearby farmer's market. Everyone had been crowding around the puppies, while Aldwin slept in his corner stall. No one else at the market seemed to want to bring home an oversized dog of indeterminate breed who was graying at the muzzle, but Harry had been thinking about getting a dog for a while. Someone to keep him company now that everyone he knew was busy being blissfully happy and in love. Besides, he was starting to gray a little around the jawline himself, so he figured they were a perfectly matched set.

Harry was just grabbing Aldwin's leash to take him into the garden patch out front when the doorbell rang.

Anyone who knew Harry or his family would have heeded the note he'd taped to the door telling them to come on inside. Maybe it was a delivery. Or a kid going door to door selling chocolate for charity.

But as he clipped on Aldwin's leash and they walked into the foyer, something told Harry it was going to be more than that. He hoped none of his family was going to be hit by an unexpected bombshell. Drake and Rosa had been through more than enough after illegally taken nude photos of her had been leaked to the press. Suzanne and Roman had also been through a rough time together while fighting a major threat to her digital security company. Alec and Cordelia had only just cemented their happily-ever-after. And their father needed to take it easy after his recent heart attack.

The very last thing Harry expected to find on his doorstep was a teenage girl.

She looked remarkably familiar. His heart actually skipped a beat when he realized he could have been looking at Molly back when they were students. The only significant difference was that this girl's hair was a lighter shade.

Aldwin was the first to greet her, pushing his muzzle into her hand. "Oh, hi there." She patted him on his neck, which was just what he was after. "Aren't you sweet?"

The girl's resemblance to Molly was already uncanny. But it was her voice that nearly knocked Harry over. There was no denying that she must be Molly's daughter.

Immediately, he started calculating. After all, they'd broken up nearly sixteen years ago, and this girl looked to be around fifteen.

Was there any chance...?

"Are you Harrison Jack Sullivan?" she asked. Aldwin leaned against her leg, as though he felt she needed protection, and her hand lay on his ruff.

"Yes," he replied, still barely able to believe the resemblance. And what might be possible. "I'm Harry."

A flicker of a smile crossed the girl's face before disappearing back into uncertainty. "Harry," she said, as though she were trying on his name for size. "I like that more than Harrison. It's not so stuffy."

He would have laughed—teenagers had a knack for knocking you down a peg or two without even trying. But how could he laugh when he couldn't stop wondering…?

He had to clear his throat. "And who are you?"

"Amelia." She bit her lip, looking more nervous than ever as she said, "Amelia Connal. Molly Connal is my mother. I'm fifteen years old. I know you used to date my mom in college." Her chin tipped up as she looked him right in the eyes. "And I think you're my father."

In mounted martial arts, Harry had the wind knocked out of him on a regular basis, and he'd taken dozens of fists to the gut over the years while goofing around with his brothers and cousins. But he'd never felt like this. Like he was fruitlessly gasping for oxygen. Like his entire world had just shifted on its axis.

Like nothing would ever be the same again.

"I have this." She took a folded piece of paper from the pocket of her jeans. "It's the results from a DNA kit I got online. See?" She handed it to him. "It says fifty percent of our DNA is a match."

Harry's hands shook as he took the paper from her. As a professor of medieval history with a particular interest in genealogy, he had been asked to write a paper on the recent explosion of DNA services that proposed not only to find out your genetic history, but also claimed to give you the chance to see into your past and discover your heritage. As part of his research for the project, he'd signed up for one of the most popular services, going so far as to check the box that would enable open sharing of his name and contact information with potential relatives. He'd enjoyed connecting with a few far-flung fourth and fifth cousins he hadn't already known about, but he'd never thought he'd find a daughter.

Or rather, that *she* would find *him*.

The information on the page couldn't be more clear:

Strength of Relationship between Amelia Connal
and Harrison Jack Sullivan
50% shared

And then one more word on the line just below that:

Father

Harry couldn't stop looking at the word, still couldn't quite process what a part of him had known the moment he'd set eyes on Amelia.

Aldwin made a low sound in his throat, one that sounded remarkably like a warning, and only then did Harry realize he was still standing frozen, alternately gaping at the paper and then at Amelia.

At his *daughter*.

How could Molly have kept this secret from him

for fifteen years? She was the last person he would ever have thought would keep a father from his child. She knew just how much family meant to him, that he would go to hell and back to keep them safe. Knew it better than nearly anyone else, in fact.

"I need to let Aldwin take care of his business," he said, surprised by how normal his voice sounded when his lungs felt as though they were being squeezed in a vise. "And then you and I should head inside so that we can talk."

She nodded, but when a burst of laughter came from inside his house, she frowned. "It sounds like there are a lot of people in there."

He'd forgotten there was an engagement party going on. Now he cursed every last person inside. All he wanted was a safe, private space for him and Amelia to talk.

Harry's life had sometimes felt like a string of momentous events—from losing his mother, to the fallout from his father checking out on his kids due to grief and guilt, to Harry needing to pick up the slack with his brothers and sister for so many years to keep his family together.

But nothing could have prepared Harry for this. For the moment when he looked at another person for the very first time and *loved*. Loved wholly and completely and unconditionally, without knowing anything more than that the teenage girl standing in front of him was *his*. And that from this moment forward, he would protect her with every last part of him.

Starting with keeping her from the prying gazes of everyone at the party.

But he couldn't ask Amelia to walk down the street with him to go talk at a coffee shop. She deserved a hell of a lot better than that from the father who had been absent her entire life, the father she'd only just found. And they couldn't go in through the back either, not when there were at least two dozen people on the deck and lawn.

"I'm hosting an engagement party for my sister Suzanne and her fiancé, and my brother Drake and his fiancée."

The unspoken words *your aunt and uncle* hung between them, along with all the other things he wanted to say to her, the questions he wanted to ask. So many that his brain felt so overcrowded and tangled up that he couldn't actually get anything straight.

"Maybe I should come back later."

Amelia was already backing out of the garden, with Aldwin straining at his leash to stick to her like glue, when a familiar voice called, "There you are." Harry's father was standing on the front stoop. "I saw the door was open and wanted to make sure Aldwin hadn't gotten out." That was when William noticed Amelia.

"Hello there."

"Hi." She stilled, one hand on the front gate latch.

"This is my father, William," Harry said without taking his eyes off his daughter.

Would he ever tire of looking at her? Would he ever feel as though he'd had enough time with her after missing the first fifteen years of her life?

"Dad—" Harry finally turned to meet his father's curious gaze. He needed his dad to know before anyone else, one parent to another. "I just found out that Amelia is my daughter."

CHAPTER TWO

"Your *daughter?*"

William looked utterly stunned as he turned to Amelia and really *looked* at her. "My God." His voice was hushed. "I should have seen the resemblance before. You have Harry's eyes, his mouth." He gripped the rail as he slowly made his way down the stairs toward her, prompting the dog to press even closer to her. William stared at her in wonder. "You're my *granddaughter.*" He sounded overwhelmed, but clearly overjoyed. "I'm your grandfather."

For the first time since Harry had opened the door, Amelia smiled. It was the prettiest ray of sunshine, and so much like her mother's smile that Harry's knees nearly buckled beneath him.

No matter how he turned things over inside his head, he couldn't believe Molly would have deliberately kept his daughter from him, no matter how awful a boyfriend he'd been.

But what other reason could there be?

After looking at Harry again and confirming just

how shell-shocked his son was, William held out his arm to Amelia. "Why don't you come inside? I know the rest of the family would love to meet you and get to know you."

Amelia looked at Harry. "Is that okay with you?"

But he couldn't stop staring at her, couldn't stop thinking, *She's mine. My daughter. I have a daughter.*

"Harry?" His father's voice was sharp enough to break through the thoughts and questions running through Harry's head at a million miles an hour. Getting stuck inside his head was one of his worst habits, according to his sister.

Harry knew he needed to get over his confusion and shock and give every ounce of his compassion and love and support to his daughter, who had just done a very brave thing with no certainty whatsoever of a positive outcome. For all Amelia knew, he might have denied her claim and tossed her out into the street.

He could read the fear on her face even now. That he didn't want her. That he would send her away.

No. He'd *never* send her away.

"I should be the one to take you in." He smiled at her, or at least tried to. At the moment, he wasn't sure he was capable of anything as clear cut as upturned lips. "I *want* to take you inside to meet your family. If that's okay with you."

Her shoulders dropped, as though she'd finally let

out the breath she'd been holding. And then she smiled, the very first smile that was his and his alone. "It's definitely okay."

As though Harry's family and friends had a sixth sense that something major was going down, all conversation stopped when he walked into the living room with Amelia between him and his father. Instinctively shifting to block her from sight, he said in a low voice, "Dad, could you ask Alec, Suzanne, and Drake to come into my study?"

His father nodded, heading into the throng as Harry gestured for Amelia to come with him down the hall, away from the party. "I'm thinking it would be good for you to meet your aunt and uncles in a more private setting."

"Okay." Her voice sounded small, unsure. "Thanks."

Throughout, Aldwin remained by her side, her personal furry sentry. It was as though the instant she'd patted his head, she'd become his responsibility.

Smart dog.

There was so much Harry wanted to say to her, and to ask, as they walked together down the hallway. So many things he wanted to know about her childhood, where she'd grown up, what she was studying in school. He didn't know anything about her, not even the basics, like her favorite color, or food, or book, or movie.

But first, he needed to ask her, "Does your mother know you're here?"

Instead of answering, she stopped at the threshold of his study, a large, vaulted room in which every wall was covered in bookshelves. "Wow. This room looks like it should be in a castle." Leather-bound books held court in his personal library alongside hardcovers and paperbacks, fiction and nonfiction, academic tomes and books of maps. Rapt, she moved toward the nearest bookshelf, running her fingers along the large leather spines of medieval battle plan reproductions.

It moved him deeply to see that his daughter was so interested in books, to know they had that in common. He hoped to find out about the dozens of other ways they might be similar—and also the ways they would be different. All the ways she was unique, brilliant, special.

Suzanne, Alec, Drake, and their father soon walked into the room. Alec shot Harry a questioning look when he saw Amelia, but Harry knew there was no way his brother would ever be prepared for this.

Amelia moved closer to Harry, and he wanted to put his arm around her to comfort her. But he didn't know if that would be okay, if there was some set amount of time that needed to pass before she felt like he was really her father, instead of a stranger she'd just met.

"It's going to be okay," he told her in a low voice. "They're all your family."

"Harry," Alec asked, voicing what every one of them was clearly wondering, "what's going on?"

Harry couldn't stop himself from putting his arm around Amelia then. Thankfully, she leaned into him, rather than away, as he said, "Amelia is my daughter." He let that huge news land for a beat before he continued. "Molly Connal, my girlfriend from college, is her mother, and Amelia found out we're related using the same online DNA testing company I signed up for earlier this year."

His siblings' eyes were all huge. Suzanne recovered first, rushing forward, then throwing her arms around Amelia. "I'm so happy to meet you! I'm Suzanne, and I swear this is one of the greatest days of my life, getting to meet my niece."

Alec moved forward next and shook her hand, obviously trying not to overwhelm Amelia with another hug. Although he held on for several long moments. "It's great to meet you, Amelia. I'm Alec."

"And I'm Drake." Harry's youngest brother went in for a hug. Though not quite as ebullient as Suzanne's, it was no less warm and welcoming.

"I've seen your picture online!" Amelia blurted when he drew back. "You're with Rosalind Bouchard."

Of course Amelia would know who Rosa was—a

fifteen-year-old would have to be seriously out of the loop not to know about the most famous former reality TV star on the planet.

"Rosa is my fiancée," Drake confirmed with a smile. "She's out in the living room. You'll meet her soon."

Seeing his family welcome Amelia one by one, without panic or cynicism, helped loosen some of the knots inside Harry. Before she met anyone else, however, they needed to nail down a few details.

"Why doesn't everyone sit down?" he said as he closed the study door. "So we can talk things through a bit."

He appreciated Suzanne's leading Amelia over to the leather love seat, with the dog keeping pace beside them. Suzanne kept her arm around Amelia, obviously recognizing some girl power wouldn't go amiss at this point. But though his sister looked to be champing at the bit to fire off questions, she managed to rein herself in as they all looked to him.

Leaning his hip against the edge of his desk—he couldn't sit, not when he was filled with this much adrenaline—Harry asked again, "Amelia, does your mother know you're here?"

She scrunched up her face, guilt written all over it. "She thinks I'm sleeping over at my friend's house."

A string of silent curses ran through Harry's head.

Of course Molly wouldn't have sent Amelia to him after all these years, especially without warning. "You need to call her and tell her where you really are."

"As long as I'm home by tomorrow at noon, she won't need to know."

"She's your mother, and we aren't going to keep either the test results, or where you are, from her." He'd been a father for all of five minutes, and he was already lecturing his daughter. "I can call her," he said in a gentler tone, "if that will be easier."

Amelia thought about it for a few seconds. "I don't know—that might be worse. I mean, since she never wanted to tell me about you, I'm thinking she wouldn't be too happy about talking to you on the phone."

Her words were like a sledgehammer to his gut. Of course Molly wouldn't want to talk to him. Too bad for his ex that he didn't give a damn what she wanted. Yes, he'd hurt her way back when. But nothing he'd done could have been bad enough for her to keep his daughter from him.

"Now that I've thought about it," Harry said, "I need to be the one to call her."

"Right now?" Amelia looked seriously panicked. She might have snuck off to find her father, but he had a feeling it had been a rare bout of rule-breaking.

"Soon." He pushed away from his desk and walked over to sit on the ottoman facing her, gently touching her hands with his. "Does she know you took the DNA test?"

She shook her head. "But after I read her diary, I had to do it."

"Molly has been writing about me in her diary?" After all these years, was she still thinking about him the way he'd never been able to stop thinking about her?

"No. I found a box of her old diaries in the attic."

Suzanne couldn't keep quiet any longer. "Your mom kept her old diaries lying around in the attic, even though you could easily have found them?"

"They weren't exactly lying around," Amelia admitted. "I had to sort of hunt for them." She looked around at everyone as if to make her case. "I needed to know who my dad was. And since she refused to ever tell me, I had to take matters into my own hands." She licked her lips, looking nervous again. "That's why as soon as I read about how she and Harry dated, I fudged her consent to do the DNA test." Her mouth took on a stubborn tilt as she turned back to Harry. "After what I read, I needed to know for sure if you were my dad."

"I can't believe Molly kept you a secret from me." Harry heard his voice as if from a distance. Despite his words, his tone was dangerously cool. Where anyone else would have been ranting, cursing, it was instinct for Harry to become more rational, not less. Losing himself in emotion had never helped anyone, and he couldn't start losing it now, even if that was the obvious route.

"All my life," Amelia said, "I assumed my father must be no good. Otherwise, why would she have kept us apart? But I still needed to know who I am, where I came from. And now that I've met you…" Amelia looked as confused and as hurt as Harry felt. "I always thought I had the best mom in the world. But all these years, I could have had you as my dad." She looked at everyone in the room. "I could have had all of you as my family."

Suzanne pulled Amelia close. "You have us now. And none of us are going anywhere, I promise."

Amelia sniffled, then pulled back. "I always wanted an aunt." She turned to Alec and Drake. "And uncles." She looked at William. "And a grandpa." And then, finally, to Harry. "And most of all, a dad." But before he could say that learning he had a daughter was the best thing that had ever happened to him, she added, "Are you sure you want to call my mom right now? I mean, I could just take the bus home and then we could come up with a plan later. Like, maybe you could show up in A Bay and accidentally bump into us on the street, and then when she sees it's you, she'll *have* to admit you're my dad. We could act like we'd only just met and be all surprised."

"A Bay?" He'd barely heard Amelia's master plan, not after hearing where she'd come from. "You took a bus all the way from Alexandria Bay today?" His gut twisted tighter. "By *yourself?*" A deep seed of fear planted itself in the middle of the emotional storm raging inside him.

"It was only forty-two bucks and five hours." She said it like teenage girls traveled that far alone with a bunch of strangers with no one to protect them all the time. "It wasn't a big deal."

Were it not for Drake moving behind Harry to put a hand on his shoulder, he wasn't sure he would have been able to control his response, for once.

"She's okay, Harry." Drake was stepping into Harry's shoes like a champ—taking on the role of keeping him from losing it the way Harry had so often helped his siblings and father. "Although," his brother said to Amelia, "how about we agree that should be the end of your solo bus trips for a while?"

Still star struck by Drake due to his relationship with Rosa, Amelia automatically nodded. "Okay. Although I don't know how I'm going to get home if I don't take the bus. I can't afford a plane ticket."

"I can fly you home on one of my planes," Alec offered.

"You have your own planes?" Amelia's eyes were huge.

"I'll be taking Amelia home myself," Harry ground out from between clenched teeth. Or, better yet, she'd stay with him instead of going back to Alexandria Bay. After all, Molly had had her first fifteen years to herself. He was due the next fifteen, at the very least.

"If you're okay hanging out with Suzanne, Drake, Alec, and my dad for a few minutes," he said to Amelia in as normal a voice as he could muster, "it's time for me to call your mother. Why don't you give me her cell phone number?"

"Okay," Amelia said, biting her lip again. "She had to go into work today, though. At Boldt Castle. I don't know if she'll pick up unless it's me."

"Then I should call from your phone to make sure she does."

Amelia's hand shook a little as she gave her cell to him, and Aldwin nestled in closer to her, putting his big head in her lap.

Harry was halfway out the door when she said, "Harry?" He turned, wishing she'd said *Dad*, even though he knew he hadn't earned it yet. "Can you tell her that I'm sorry I did all of this behind her back?"

His stomach twisted tight at the regret—and the love—in her voice. "Don't worry, Amelia. Everything is going to be okay."

He'd move heaven and earth to make sure of that.

CHAPTER THREE

Harry closed himself into his bedroom upstairs. Party guests were gathered outside the window in the backyard, but they were all a blur. Scrolling through Amelia's list of contacts, he found *Mom* and pressed the call button with a shaking hand.

Molly picked up after one ring. "Amelia? Is everything okay, sweetie?"

The shock of hearing her voice after so many years of hearing it only in his dreams made him momentarily speechless. "It's not Amelia. It's Harry. Harry Sullivan."

Molly went so silent on the other end that he almost thought their connection had been severed. Obviously stunned, she asked, "How do you have Amelia's phone?"

"She found me." He barely recognized his own voice, it was so strangled with repressed fury and frustration. "She's here in the city."

Molly gasped. "Amelia is in the city?" Shock reverberated through every word.

"She took a bus here. Five hours. All by herself."

Just saying the words riled him up all over again. "Anything could have happened to her."

"She took the *bus* to the city?" He could hear how shaken she was. "Is she okay?"

"She's fine, thank God."

"Put her on. I need to talk to my daughter."

"*Our* daughter. And I'll put her on as soon as you and I are done." His gut was churning as he said, "Why the hell did you hide my daughter from me?" He could no longer pretend to keep his cool. "How could you do that to me? And to her?"

"Wait…what are you saying?" She sounded completely confused, even more than she'd been when he'd told her who was calling. "How could you possibly think Amelia is your daughter?"

"She read your old diary, Molly. She read what you wrote about me."

"I did write about you and how we dated, but I never said you were her father. You're not. You can't be."

He couldn't believe she was trying to deny it. "I have proof. She took a DNA test, and I showed up as matching fifty percent of her genetic markers."

"You might have a piece of paper that says that, but it has to be wrong. Some kind of horrible joke someone is playing on her. She's never been bullied before, but maybe something has changed at school that I don't know about. Maybe she mentioned your name to someone after reading my diary and they thought it would be funny to mail her false test results."

Whatever Harry had expected, it wasn't this. Not just an out-and-out denial, but Molly's utter refusal that he was Amelia's father. Worse still, she was somehow managing to plant doubts in his head, even though he was holding the DNA test result.

"Finding out I have a teenage daughter is no joke."

"Of course it isn't, but I'm telling you, it's not possible."

"She's mine, Molly." Hadn't his father said Amelia had his eyes, his mouth? And hadn't she fit right in with his siblings, as though she'd always been a part of the family? Always been a Sullivan? *"Mine."*

Molly made a frustrated sound into the phone. "I need to come get Amelia, and once I'm there, we'll figure out how she could have gotten her hands on this mistaken DNA test result."

"It's no mistake," he insisted. "The timing of everything is exactly right—it's been fifteen years and nine months since we were last together."

"No, we had already broken up when I got pregnant." She was just as insistent. "She's *not* yours."

"We'll do another paternity test—and then you won't be able to deny the truth." Harry almost never raised his voice. He'd always been the calm one, the person everyone could count on to be reasonable. But now he was practically shouting into Amelia's phone.

"Don't you dare do anything until I get there." Molly's shock shifted to a fierce protectiveness. "I get that you think I've kept Amelia from you her entire life. But I swear I haven't. And even if you don't believe me, when it comes to my daughter, I will protect her *no matter what.*" Her voice was slightly softer as she added, "I'm sorry you aren't her father, Harry. But I really think it's best if we go over everything in person rather than on the phone so that there's no chance of your misunderstanding. And even more than that, I need to see my daughter and know that she's okay. Where do you live?"

The thought of seeing Molly again, of her walking into his house, was so strange, he couldn't begin to imagine how it would feel.

He gave her the address. Then she said, "I'll be there as fast as I can safely manage the drive. Now, could I please talk to my daughter?"

The last thing he wanted was to let Molly off the hook. He wanted to force her to tell him everything right that second. But despite how upset he was, he also understood how desperate she must be to talk to Amelia—and to come here to see for herself that she was okay. And Amelia must be a bundle of nerves waiting to find out how their call was going.

"I'll take the phone out to her now." As Harry walked down to his study, he could hear laughter coming from the room. He'd never appreciated his family more than he did right at this moment, when they were going out of their way to get over their own shock at meeting Amelia so that they could help settle her nerves. "She's with Alec, Suzanne, Drake and my father."

"You called everyone to come over as soon as Amelia showed up?"

"They were already here. We're celebrating Drake's and Suzanne's engagements today. They'll both be getting married later this year."

Despite the knots twisting him up at the doubts Molly had managed to plant inside him, he smiled at Amelia as he walked into the study. "Your mom is going to drive here tonight, so you'll be seeing her soon. Here she is."

Amelia took the phone from him and walked over to the window for a little more privacy. "Mom—"

Everyone in the room could hear Molly exclaim how glad she was that Amelia was okay, then say that she had scared her half to death by getting on that bus.

Amelia's shoulders slumped. "I know I shouldn't have taken the bus so far by myself. I'm really sorry." Then her shoulders moved back slightly. "But I needed to know who my dad is! And he's great. They all are."

Everyone in the room raised their eyebrows as Molly told Amelia that she'd explain everything once she got there, then all but hollered that she still should have told her what she was doing—and that she was grounded. *Forever.*

Amelia slumped again. "I already said I wouldn't do it again—you don't need to ground me."

Whatever Molly said next was at a lower volume, but Harry could just make out the words *I love you so much* from across the room.

"Love you too, Mom. See you when you get here." Amelia slid the phone into her back pocket, then turned toward the group, obviously not realizing they had been able to hear their conversation. "She's pretty mad."

Harry moved to her side. "She's just glad you're okay." He smiled at her, his heart fuller than it had ever been for the teenager who had instantly become the center of his world. "I am too."

When she smiled back, regardless of the doubts Molly had put into his head, he opened his arms to Amelia...and was so damned glad when she walked into them and lay her head on his chest.

"I'm so happy you found me, Amelia."

"Me too."

He held on for a long time. But it would never be long enough. He already knew that.

When he reluctantly let her go, he tried to corral his spinning, spiraling thoughts into a straight line. She had to be hungry, thirsty, and wondering where she was going to be staying. "How about I show you your bedroom while your aunt, uncles, and grandfather clear out the party? And then we can get you something to eat and drink?"

"I am pretty starved," she said, rubbing her hand over her stomach. "I can't go that long without food or Mom says I get grumpy."

"Just like Suzanne," Drake drawled. "It's a seriously bad idea to ever let her blood sugar get too low."

Suzanne rolled her eyes, then said to Amelia, "Bet you didn't figure you'd have a couple of uncles like these guys to deal with."

"I think they're both awesome! All of you are."

"Right back at you, Amelia," Alec said with a grin. "Welcome to the family."

And as Harry picked up her backpack and took her upstairs to one of the guest bedrooms, with Aldwin pressed so close to her that she could barely walk in a straight line, she beamed the whole way.

Already a Sullivan through and through.

CHAPTER FOUR

Molly had forgotten how dark and how quiet this part of the city could be in the middle of the night. Her memories of living in New York City were always bright and colorful, especially after she'd met Harry. For the first time in her life, she had truly felt alive.

All because she'd fallen head over heels in love.

The first time she'd met Harry, she'd been in the university library, down deep in the special collections stacks where the most valuable books were stored. Books so old you needed a special pass and gloves to protect the pages. She was trying to get a book about Boldt Castle on the top shelf, but couldn't reach it. That was when Harry had walked into the room, moved behind her, and pulled it out.

Even at eighteen, he'd already been so rugged and strong. It fit perfectly that he'd been studying the medieval period, and it had been a thrill to find someone as excited about history as she was. They came at history from different angles—he focused primarily on battles, whereas she was interested in what love and family had looked like in the past—but that had only made it more exciting as they not only learned from each other, but also sparked new ideas during their discussions.

It was always so amazing when they were together. Harry was not only the sexiest man, he was also utterly devoted to his family in a way that she'd never known anyone could be. Just looking at him had made her smile, and when he touched her...

Though she hadn't seen him in nearly sixteen years, just thinking of his touch made her heart race.

She shook her head to clear away a vivid picture of Harry levered over her, taking her places she hadn't known she could go—higher, sweeter, brighter than anything she'd ever felt before. But once the image took hold, it was nearly impossible to shake away. Especially when every man she'd been with after him had seemed like nothing more than a cut-rate consolation prize.

At eighteen, he'd seemed like her knight in shining armor. Literally, even, when he jousted at historical reenactments. She couldn't believe how lucky she was to find him—her, a girl who had never really known love, ending up with a guy who believed so strongly in family. She'd dreamed of her happily-ever-after, of never being lonely again, of finally mattering to someone and trusting they would never let her down.

But nothing was ever that simple, was it?

Right from the start, Harry frequently had to cancel their dates. His family needed him constantly, especially his father. Molly loved how important family was to him, and because she didn't want to admit to herself that it hurt to always come last, she told herself it was no big deal. Throughout her life, her parents had moved from one remote village to another while working to set up freshwater systems. Molly had traveled with them until she'd been old enough to attend boarding school in first grade.

Just as she knew how important her parents' work was, she couldn't let herself be upset with Harry for canceling on her when she knew how badly his family needed him. Especially given how he always tried so hard to carve out time for her from his busy schedule. In addition to his classes, he frequently needed to head to a parent-teacher meeting with one of Suzanne's or Drake's high school teachers, or rush off to a bar to make sure his brother Alec made it home safely, or spend weekends and school breaks helping his father in the Adirondacks.

Harry had never talked that much about what his father was going through, but due to William Sullivan's massive fame as a painter, Molly at least knew the bare bones of the story—Harry's father had lost his wife when the kids were very young and had never gotten over it.

And now…

Now Harry thought *he* was Amelia's father.

For the past four and a half hours of the drive from Alexandria Bay, she'd gone through every deep-breathing meditation technique she knew to get her hands to stop shaking on the steering wheel. Unfortunately, the tremors were still moving through her. In fact, by now full-body shivers were racking her frame, making her teeth chatter.

Hearing Harry's voice over the phone earlier that night had been the biggest surprise of her life. Until he'd shocked her a thousand times more by accusing her of keeping his daughter from him for fifteen years.

God, no, she would never have done that.

Never.

★ ★ ★

Freshman year, Columbia University…

Harry had promised to make Molly's birthday a night she would never forget. They'd been dating for five months, and for Molly, every night they spent together was already incredibly special, even if they were simply bent over their laptops working on papers. As long as she was with Harry, she was happy.

He'd told her he was taking her to some of his favorite places in the city, places he said he wanted to share with her. She'd been looking forward to the evening for weeks and had barely been able to concentrate in her classes that day.

Molly's parents hadn't remembered her birthday. She hadn't gotten a phone call, or a letter, or even a card. She wasn't surprised, as they'd forgotten more birthdays than they'd remembered over the years.

But Harry wouldn't let her down.

She spent an hour on her hair, her makeup. Earlier that week, she'd splashed out on new lingerie. As she was at Columbia on a scholarship, it was money she didn't have, but it would be worth it just to see the heat leap into Harry's eyes when he stripped her out of it.

Mere minutes before he would be arriving to pick her up, she slipped on her prettiest dress, a sky blue that he said matched her eyes, the soft jersey fabric skimming her curves and floating around her legs with every step she took in her inexpensive but lovely heeled sandals.

She'd never felt more beautiful, or been so full of anticipation.

Seven p.m. came, and she smiled as she looked out the window of her tiny dorm room at the street below. Harry would be ringing the bell any moment now. Who knew, maybe they wouldn't even make it out of her room. Not for a while, anyway, until she'd pulled him close and showed him just how happy she was to celebrate her birthday with him.

Fifteen minutes passed. Then thirty. And still, Harry hadn't arrived. He wasn't responding to her texts or picking up her calls either.

Had something happened to him?

Her heart was in her throat as she called his family home, where he still lived with Suzanne and Drake so that he could watch over his younger siblings. She'd been to the house several times over the past months and knew his sister and youngest brother. She'd met Alec once, but had never met their father, as he was always at his lake home.

She prayed Harry was okay. She knew he'd never forget her birthday. Hopefully, it was just that she'd gotten their meeting time, or place, wrong.

Drake picked up their home phone. "Is Harry there?" she asked. "We were supposed to meet tonight—" She left off that it was for her birthday. "—but he's really late, and I'm starting to worry."

"He didn't tell you?"

"Tell me what?"

"Harry went to Summer Lake to see Dad."

In Drake's voice, she could hear sadness over his father's problems—but also pity for her. Almost as though he'd guessed that she'd been waiting for Harry in her prettiest dress and heels, watching out the window, wanting so badly to believe in him, to count on him.

Wanting so badly to come first, for once. On her birthday.

"Oh." She didn't know what else to say. Not when any other words might come out as a sob.

"There's no cell reception out there," Drake said, "but if you want to try to reach Harry, I can give you my dad's landline."

Her hands shook as she dialed William Sullivan's number. The phone rang so many times she wasn't sure anyone would pick up. Finally, she heard Harry's voice. "Sullivan residence."

"Harry." Her voice was breathless, and suddenly she didn't know what to say. "It's Molly."

"Where did you get this number?"

"Drake gave it to me." She hated the way the words shook, but nothing about this night had gone the way she'd imagined it would. A dream that was quickly turning into a nightmare. "He said you went to see your dad."

"Things are bad here." When Harry didn't apologize for missing her birthday, she realized she'd been wrong. He must have forgotten.

"What happened?" Somehow, she managed to keep the conversation going, if only because Harry sounded so desolate. As though he'd finally reached the end of his tether.

"I got a call from my father's business partner. When he didn't show up to work, she got worried and called me. I found him passed out drunk on the kitchen floor."

"Oh, Harry, I'm so sorry."

"My mother died today." He cursed, something she'd never heard him do before. "Not actually today— it's the anniversary of her death. My dad swore he wasn't going to fall apart this year. He promised me he was getting over it. I should have known better, should have known he's never going to get over losing her."

It was not only the most Harry had ever said to her about his father, it was also the only time she'd ever felt him falter under the pressure of shouldering so much responsibility for his family's happiness. Before tonight, he'd always seemed so strong, so capable, as though what he did for everyone was no big deal.

"Why didn't you tell me what day it was?" Molly asked.

"What good would it have done?"

It would have brought us closer. It would have shown that you trusted me with your heart the way I've trusted mine with you.

Harry was the only one to whom she'd admitted feeling abandoned by her parents. Only to find out he'd stayed locked up so tight that even as he'd told her of his plans for her birthday, he hadn't thought she should know the significance of the date.

Despite her own hurt feelings, everything inside her ached for him, for his father, for his siblings. Though she wasn't very close to her parents, she couldn't imagine how difficult it would be to lose one of them.

"If I had known," she said softly, "I would have been there for you. And I wouldn't have let you plan a birthday celebration for me tonight."

Another curse came through the phone line as he obviously realized he'd forgotten all about their celebration.

"It's okay—" she began.

"No, it isn't. I love you, Molly, you know how much I love you, and I'm giving you as much as I can, but…"

But.

The word ricocheted through her head, her heart, as the rest of whatever he'd been about to say fell away.

All Molly's life, she'd been a *but* to the people who said they loved her. Deep inside her heart, she knew this was the moment it was over. Harry would never truly be hers. She would never get the fairy tale. Nothing could possibly be more clear than *I love you, but...*

Even then, though, she couldn't stand to let him go. Couldn't give up on her dreams of a love that could transcend anything.

"I understand that your family needs you," she said, trying to sound reasonable. Trying to act as though she wasn't desperate not to lose him. "I could never live with myself if I kept you from them. You were right to go help your father tonight."

"It's not just for tonight." Another blow landed on her heart. "I'm going to have to stay here at the lake with him until he's back on his feet. I've got to keep an eye on him and also step in to help run his construction company."

"What about your classes?" But both of them knew she wasn't just asking about school. She was also asking, *What about us?*

"I'll have to take an incomplete and make up the work for the last few weeks of school. This summer, probably." Most students wouldn't be able to do this, but Harry was so bright that his professors would likely bend over backward to help him finish his first-year courses.

"I'll help you any way I can," she offered. "I can even come to the lake tonight. I'll ask around the dorm and see if I can borrow someone's car."

"Molly." The way he said her name sent chills

through her. It was almost worse than hearing *I love you, but...* "You deserve better."

She didn't think it was possible for her heart to keep breaking. But every new sentence out of Harry's mouth proved her wrong, made her feel as though she would shatter into a million pieces.

She wanted to throw her phone out the window. Wanted to crawl into bed and pull her pillow over her head. Wanted to rewind back to earlier when she'd felt so happy, so hopeful.

But for once she knew she couldn't hide from the truth.

"What are you saying?" she asked, her voice barely above a whisper. "Are you breaking up with me?"

"I can't ask you to keep waiting for me, for my life to stop being so crazy." His words fell like hammers on her brain. "You should have broken up with me a long time ago."

Other girls would probably have given up on him after being stood up at least a half-dozen times. But she'd been so desperate for love that even now he had to be the one to end it, because she would have turned herself inside out to keep holding on to him. She would have kept convincing herself that having part of a little was better than having nothing at all.

And yet, even when he was holding up a mirror and forcing her to see the truth, even after he'd told her he couldn't give her what she needed, that there wasn't any of him left for her—she still might have begged. Until she heard the crashing sound that echoed across the phone line, one so loud that it made her gasp.

"Harry?"

"It's my father. I need to go." The line went dead.

★ ★ ★

The next day, Molly had been hit with the world's worst cramps. It had been a relief to have a reason to crawl into bed and curl up into a ball. To tell herself that getting her period was why she was overly emotional and couldn't stop crying. She'd be fine without Harry—she'd been alone before and she could do it again.

Only, as one day dragged into the next, then one week finally crawled into two, she couldn't deny that she'd never felt more alone. All because Harry had shown her how good it could be when she *wasn't* alone.

So when some girls who also lived on her dormitory floor asked her to go out with them, and knowing that if she stayed in she'd only torment herself with more memories of Harry, she'd agreed.

Molly had thought her life had changed forever the night Harry dumped her. But yet again, she'd been wrong, because it was at a party full of strangers—two weeks *after* she and Harry split up—that everything had actually changed.

The night she'd conceived her daughter with a stranger who hadn't wanted anything at all to do with them.

CHAPTER FIVE

Present day...

Molly sighed for what had to be the hundredth time as she drove the residential streets that led to Harry's home. She wasn't at all surprised that he'd fulfilled his promise as a brilliant academic and scholar. Harry was one of the smartest people she'd ever met, though he hadn't ever bragged or lorded it over anyone.

She was proud of the life she'd built for herself and Amelia. She'd saved every last penny to buy their tiny bungalow just off Alexandria Bay's main street and had filled their home with bright colors on the walls and fabrics and rugs. Still, how could her daughter not compare their little house to the elegant brownstones in Harry's neighborhood without finding it wanting?

She hated to think how heartbroken Amelia was going to be when Molly told her Harry wasn't her father. All during the drive, she had been kicking herself for not having sat down with her before now to explain things. When her daughter was younger, it had been easy for Molly to justify sweeping information about Amelia's father under the rug. After all, what young child wanted to hear that she'd been born after a one-night stand with a guy who turned out to be a total jerk? Molly prayed fifteen was old enough for Amelia to finally hear the truth without it hurting her.

As for how Harry would react after he heard Molly's story? After he realized that he and Amelia couldn't possibly be related despite a piece of paper that somehow said otherwise?

Molly was afraid he'd be devastated. Because how could anyone in their right mind not want Amelia to be theirs? She was the perfect kid. As perfect as any teenager with raging hormones could be, in any case. Thankfully, she didn't have any of that world-weariness that plenty of girls her age exhibited. Amelia didn't spend hours slapping on makeup or trying to convince Molly to let her wear inappropriate clothes that would make her look older.

Molly pulled up in front of Harry's house, her heart racing. As she got out of the car, she refused to check her hair, which she'd thrown into a ponytail during the drive, or the dark jeans and loose green sweater she'd been wearing at work when he'd called. Why would she, when this was as far from a social call as it got?

Harry's house was dark, apart from the porch light and another light deeper in. Without yet having been inside his home, she could guess the room where he'd likely be waiting for her. His study, where he'd be surrounded by leather-bound books, and probably with a full suit of armor in the corner. Exactly the life he'd dreamed of having back when they were in college.

The life she had dreamed of sharing with him.

Her legs shook as she walked up the stairs, and she felt lightheaded by the time she knocked on his door. Molly had always had a terrible fear that if she and Harry were ever in the same room again, she'd take one look at him and either launch herself into his arms...or fall completely apart. She was about to find out which it would be.

She heard footsteps and then the lock turning.

"Molly."

The years fell away as she stared at him, momentarily unable to speak, or think, or breathe.

"Come inside." While she felt like an open book, gaping at him on his doorstep, she couldn't read a thing in his tone, his expression.

She followed him into the foyer. "Is Amelia still awake?"

"She went to bed around eleven, after my family finally cleared out." His voice softened, warmed, when he spoke of Amelia, and even his lips began to curve up into a smile.

Seeing that—knowing that—made everything inside Molly's chest clench tight. If only he *was* Amelia's father...

"I need to see her, even though she's already asleep," she said in as steady a voice as she could manage, given that her emotions felt more high-strung than they had ever been. And that was saying something, considering what a mess she'd been in those early postpartum months as a single mother trying to take care of a baby while living on a shoestring.

Harry led her through the foyer, past the living room and kitchen, then up a wide set of stairs. His voice pitched low, he said, "She's in here."

Carefully easing open the bedroom door, Molly crept into where her daughter was fast asleep in a plush-looking bed. An enormous wolfhound mix was lying across the foot of the mattress. Of course Harry would have a dog like this—the perfect academic's companion.

From the moment Harry had phoned to say Amelia was here, though he'd assured Molly that her daughter was fine, she hadn't been able to stop the worst-case scenarios from playing inside her head. So many horrible things could have happened to Amelia on a solo bus trip from Alexandria Bay to the city.

Only now that Molly saw Amelia safe and sound, even smiling a little in her sleep, could she finally release the breath she'd been holding.

The dog watched Molly carefully as she bent to press a kiss to Amelia's cheek. "Love you, sweet girl."

Her daughter shifted, but didn't wake up. The dog stared at Molly, unblinking, for several seconds then, when he deemed she wasn't a threat, laid his muzzle on Amelia's feet.

Without thinking, Molly turned to smile with relief at Harry. When he didn't smile back, she remembered she had a heck of a lot of explaining to do.

And that he wasn't going to want to hear any of it.

After tiptoeing out of the room and shutting the door, Molly felt as though she were heading to the gallows, rather than simply following Harry downstairs.

"That's Aldwin, with Amelia," Harry said. "He hasn't left her side since the moment she arrived."

Beyond nervous, Molly found herself babbling, "His name is perfect for him—he already seems like her old friend."

Harry stopped on the stairs. "You know that *Aldwin* means *old friend*?"

Too late, she realized what she'd just given away. "I tried to keep up my studies after college. And I always found the medieval period particularly fascinating." Which was true. It was also true that the main reason she'd dug deeper into medieval history was because it was a secret link to Harry.

"If you still drink peppermint tea," he said once they were in the kitchen, "I can make you a cup."

It was funny—and by *funny* she meant *not at all funny*—how something like remembering the kind of tea she used to drink when they were together could mean so much. But she couldn't do this, couldn't just sit and make polite conversation when nothing added up.

"Harry, I'm sorry, but you can't be Amelia's father."

"Yes, I am." Reaching into his pocket, he pulled out a piece of paper and handed it to her. "It's all there in black and white."

Unfolding it, she saw the information printed on letterhead from an online ancestry DNA test company. The company was claiming that Harry shared fifty percent of Amelia's DNA.

Molly honestly wasn't sure how Amelia had come to get this, or how anyone could think playing such a horrible prank on her daughter could ever be funny.

She put the paper on the granite kitchen counter, steeling herself for the story she was about to tell. One she wasn't proud of, but wouldn't take back for anything. Not when Amelia had come to be hers because of it.

"First of all," she said, "when you and I were together, we were always used protection."

"Protection can fail."

"I know it can," she said, "but it didn't. Not with us."

"It must have."

"It didn't." She was as certain as he was. More so, because she actually had the facts. "The night we broke up, I got my period. It was the worst one of my life, with such severe cramps I couldn't even get out of bed."

"Molly—"

"Please, let me get this out. All of it, so that you'll finally understand." Her head was pounding like she had a hangover, though she hadn't had a drink, and her mouth was bone dry. "Two weeks after we broke up, fourteen days after my period started, I went to a party, got drunk, and...I slept with a stranger."

With another Columbia student who had looked like Harry. A poor man's version, anyway. He'd been so attentive that night, giving her everything she craved, making her feel as though she was the only person who mattered. At least, until the deed was done and he'd kicked her out to do an early-morning walk of shame back to her dorm in her dress and heels.

She made herself look Harry square in the eyes. "I was too drunk to remember to use protection, and two weeks later when my next period was late, I did a pregnancy test. All the dates line up perfectly for her birthday."

She expected Harry to look devastated. Especially given that over the phone, he'd seemed hell-bent on being Amelia's father. Now that she'd laid out the full truth for him, why didn't he look like his whole world had just caved in?

Finally, he spoke. "Aunt Mary didn't realize she was pregnant with the twins for the same reason."

"Your Aunt Mary?" It had been a heck of an evening, but though Molly knew she was nowhere near at her best, she should still be able to follow his train of thought. "Why are you bringing her up now?"

"Because she went through the same thing you did. Not," he clarified, "the getting drunk and sleeping with a stranger part. But I definitely remember hearing Aunt Mary say that she'd gotten her period, or what she thought was her period—and then finding out not long afterward that she had already been pregnant with Sophie and her twin sister, Lori." He let his words land—along with the utter, breath-stealing shock that came with them—before adding, "She said it doesn't happen all the time, but that it isn't totally unheard of either."

Molly felt herself reeling, both physically and emotionally. It wasn't until Harry's hands curled around hers to hold her steady that she realized she had been about to drop.

"But..." She swallowed hard as she thought about the implications of what Harry was saying. "Everyone was so sure—the nurses, my doctor. I *never* thought in a million years she could be yours, not even all those times I wished she could have been. Instead of his."

"You wished Amelia was mine?"

But Molly couldn't think straight, couldn't worry about what she'd just admitted to Harry, when everything she'd believed to be true was suddenly in question.

"I..." He led her over to one of the kitchen stools, and when he let go of her hands, she dropped her head into them. "I don't know what to think right now." Her words were slightly muffled by her hands, but her voice was still clear enough. "I heard what you just said, and I know you wouldn't lie to me about your aunt." Molly lifted her head and looked at Harry, at the man she'd once loved with everything she was. The man she'd been so heartbroken to lose. The man she'd never thought she'd see again. "What if it's true? What if I was *already* pregnant when I went to that party? What if Amelia really *is* yours?" She felt both bleak—and desperately hopeful—all at the same time. "That means her father would have wanted her after all."

"Did you tell him?" Harry asked. "The other guy, the one you thought got you pregnant?"

"Of course I did. I would never willingly have kept

her from her father, or her father from her."

Harry had to believe her. He had to see that she would never have done something like this to him on purpose, and certainly not as retribution for breaking her heart. "Everything fit just right, from getting my period after our breakup, and then having unprotected sex with him exactly when I thought I would have been ovulating. Even the doctor I went to confirmed that must be my date of conception. So I went to the guy's residence hall and found him. He barely remembered me. Didn't even know my name. I felt like such an idiot. Such a cliché, the heartbroken college freshman getting drunk, ending up in some stranger's bed, then finding out she's pregnant. But I couldn't keep the truth from him."

"What did he do?"

"He told me to get rid of it. Or else. It turned out that he came from an important family, and he had been in this situation before. His family had paid the other girl to have an abortion, but I couldn't do that, couldn't let them pressure me. I had to get away from him and go somewhere they wouldn't find me— wouldn't find Amelia. He didn't know my last name, so I figured if I went far enough, we would be in the clear."

"Who is he?" Harry growled out the words.

"It doesn't matter." And if the DNA test was right,

it really didn't.

A moment later, he reached for one of the cloth napkins in a bowl on the island and pressed it to her cheek.

"Harry? What are you doing?"

"You're crying."

She lifted a hand to her face, and her fingers came away wet. She'd been so overwhelmed by going back in time and recounting some of the hardest days of her life, on top of the mind-blowing thought that Amelia might actually be Harry's, that she hadn't even realized she was crying.

Suddenly unable to hold back the torrent of emotion inside of her a single second more, she reached for the cloth, putting it over her face as the waterfalls came.

The very last thing she'd wanted to do was fall apart in front of him, but it didn't seem she had a choice. Her body, her brain, her heart, simply couldn't do anything else.

CHAPTER SIX

From the moment Harry had opened his front door to Molly—and especially now that he'd heard her side of the story and knew she couldn't possibly be trying to pull one over on him—it felt as though a fire were burning throughout his entire body. Every vein, every cell overheated. Because despite the emotions roiling through him over the story she'd just told him, he couldn't help but notice that she was even more beautiful now than she'd been at eighteen, her curves more pronounced, her features fuller, her eyes a deeper blue. And he found himself breathing her in, that tantalizing scent he'd never forgotten.

If only he hadn't pushed Molly away in college—if only he hadn't been so convinced he couldn't be enough for her when his family was pulling him in so many different directions—none of this would have happened. Not only losing Molly, but also missing out on the first fifteen years of his daughter's life.

Harry's chest ached with the realization of what he'd lost. What *all* of them had lost. Thank God Amelia had done the DNA test, then been brave enough to come and find him. Just as her mother had been brave enough to leave Columbia University when she became pregnant, before some rich punk and his family could pressure her into giving up her baby.

"Molly."

He couldn't stop himself from putting his hands over hers again, not when it felt so right. As right as it had been in college when he'd been so sure she was the one for him. Back when he'd believed that he and Molly would have the fairy tale. That there would never be the darkness or sorrow or anger that had been in his parents' marriage. That they would never hurt each other in the deepest ways two people could.

"Please." Her sobs tore at his already shredded heart. "Don't cry. We'll figure this out. All of it."

As she made an effort to stop, her chest hitched once, then twice, then again. Finally, she ran the napkin over her face, the fabric crumpled in her hand. "I didn't mean to do that, to fall apart in your kitchen. I just keep thinking about all the things that could have happened to Amelia today without me there to look out for her, without my even knowing where she was."

Drake had been Harry's voice of reason in the study this afternoon. Now it was Harry's turn to say, "You can't let yourself go to all those worst-case places inside your head. She's okay."

"But is she really? She made it here unscathed, thank God, but she grew up without a dad. All because it never occurred to me that you could possibly be her father. I swear, if I had thought there was even the barest chance, I would have come to you and said something."

"If only I'd been there for you instead of breaking things off—"

"You were burning the candle at all ends," she said, cutting off his attempts to verbally rewind time. "You were working through to sunrise most nights just to try to keep up with your classwork. The absolute last thing you needed was a needy girlfriend getting in your way. Not when you already had too much on your plate. Not when you were barely keeping everyone together. Your family would have fallen apart without you, Harry. If not for you, I don't think they would have been here at your house today celebrating together. And I would never have forgiven myself if that happened—if your family had fallen to pieces because I was in your life. Not when I knew how it would break you to lose them."

"Don't you know it broke me to lose *you*, Molly?" He hadn't planned to say any of this, but he couldn't stop the emotional words from coming. "Only to find out that I didn't just lose the love of my life, I almost lost out on ever knowing my daughter. All because I had my priorities wrong."

"I loved that you love your family so much." He was amazed that, even now, she didn't seem to blame him, nor would she let him blame himself. "That family means everything to you. I've never known anyone like you—who puts their family first, no matter the cost to themselves. Especially when my parents are the opposite. When I became a mother, I realized how much I had learned from you. So many times when I felt confused and overwhelmed, I asked myself, *What would Harry do right now?* You love your family without conditions, without boundaries, without ego. Exactly the way I love Amelia. And I will never apologize for that."

He wished it could be so simple to absolve himself of guilt over the far-reaching consequences of his actions. Consequences he could never have imagined, not in his wildest dreams.

"We need to do a second DNA test. First thing tomorrow, so that we can be one hundred percent certain that I *am* Amelia's father."

"I agree," Molly said. But then she frowned. "For years, I've been trying to figure out when I should tell her about her father—about the man I *thought* was her father. But I never wanted to say anything that might make her doubt how much I wanted her, or how much I love her."

"She would never doubt those things, Molly. Even after only one evening with her, I can say that with absolute certainty. You're the center of her world, and she knows she's the center of yours. Nothing you say to her about your past is going to change that."

"But what if she looks at me differently after I tell her that I had unprotected, drunk sex with a stranger when I was only a few years older than she is now?"

Harry's chest tightened, not only at the thought of Molly in such a vulnerable position with someone who hadn't cared about her—but also from envisioning his daughter ever being in a similar position.

"If anyone dares treat her like that, I'll destroy him." Harry had to force himself to unclench his fists. "But you're underestimating her if you think hearing your story is going to make her look at you differently."

"I hope so," she said in a soft voice. "But what about you?"

"Everything *is* different now." And he had a feeling it wasn't going to be easy to unpack his feelings over both his and Molly's roles in what had happened. But he knew one thing with absolute certainty. "No matter what happened in college, you've done a remarkable job raising Amelia."

The last thing he expected was for her face to crumple again.

"Once the DNA test comes back tomorrow, once we know for sure that she's yours," she said, "I'm going to do absolutely everything I can to make sure you and Amelia can start to know each other and create your own special moments, your own memories. So that she can have the father I know she's longed for her entire life. And for you..." She reached for his hand, without seeming to realize she'd done it. "For you to get to know the most wonderful girl in the entire world. Even if it means quitting my job and moving here so that you can be together."

He knew he should be jumping at her offer, probably even making her put it in writing so that his lawyer could take it to a family-court judge as proof of her intentions, just in case. But it had been a hell of a long day for both of them, long enough that he wasn't at all sure they were capable of thinking straight. Because as much as he wanted Amelia here in the city with him from this moment forward, he also knew the last thing any fifteen-year-old wanted was to be uprooted from her friends and school and life.

Finding her father out of the blue was change enough.

"We'll figure out everything tomorrow," he promised as he took their mugs and put them in the sink. "Let's go to bed."

He didn't realize how the words sounded until two

spots of pink appeared on her cheeks.

"I wasn't sure if you'd want me to stay here."

"Of course I do. You're Amelia's mother. Where else would you go?" This wasn't easy for either of them, but they needed to find a way to make it work. Whatever it took. "I've made up the room across from Amelia's for you."

"I think I could just lay my head right here on this island and fall asleep," she said, obviously trying to cover for her reaction. "But your guest bed would be a lot more comfortable."

The very last thing in the world either of them should be thinking about was sharing a bed. It figured, then, that he couldn't *stop* thinking about it as she got her overnight bag out of her car, then followed him up the stairs.

"Good night, Molly."

Even exhausted and wrung out by a day that had been crazier than any other, Molly was still the most radiantly beautiful woman he'd ever seen as she said, "Good night, Harry."

* * *

Harry was too wound up to sleep. So just as he'd done his whole life when he needed to escape his thoughts and emotions, he decided to work. He should have finished the draft of the book he was writing about medieval knights six months ago, but he'd hit a wall halfway through and hadn't been able to find his way forward. While he wasn't pleased to be struggling with his work, perhaps focusing on battle strategy tonight would help settle him into a more rational space.

One where he could think more clearly about Molly and Amelia and what the future was going to look like from here on out.

As soon as he opened his laptop, an instant message from Alec popped up at the top of his screen. Harry should have guessed his family would be waiting to hear from him. And maybe that was the real reason he'd gone online. Not to escape in his work, but to be able to turn to someone he loved the way they'd always turned to him whenever their lives went sideways.

Alec: Molly show up yet?

Harry: About an hour ago. She honestly didn't know Amelia was mine.

But she had confessed that she'd wished Amelia *was* his daughter. Hearing that had meant so much to him. It wouldn't make up for the years they'd lost, but at the very least, he was glad to know Molly thought he would have been a good father.

Alec: How the hell could she not think that?

Harry: It's complicated, but I believe her. So will you, once I explain. It's too late tonight to go into it all, so you'll have to trust me on it for now.

Harry wasn't planning to give his family all the nitty-gritty details, but he would tell them enough to understand why Molly wasn't to blame for Amelia only just now appearing in their lives.

Alec: From what I remember about Molly, it was hard to believe she would have kept you and Amelia apart. In a strange way, this actually makes more sense.

Clearly, Alec losing his business partner, falling in love with Cordelia, and abandoning his career as an aviation mogul to become a chef had changed his brother deeply. Enough that Alec was willing to see there could be more to the situation than what lay on the surface.

Harry: We're going to do another DNA test tomorrow to make absolutely sure she's mine.

Alec: She is. I have a medical friend who can help.

Harry smiled. Alec wanted Amelia in the family just as badly as the rest of them. If there was even the slightest chance that she wasn't…

No, he couldn't let himself think that. Couldn't find

his daughter one night and lose her the next.

Harry: Thanks for checking in.

Alec: You looked after me more times than I can count. Now it's my turn. Whatever you need, I'm here.

Harry didn't need his brother to thank him for anything he'd done. They were family. No other reasons were needed. And yet, after Molly had yanked the lid off such a huge box of memories tonight, it helped to hear it.

Especially when Harry had made some pretty big confessions of his own. Not only that she'd been the love of his life, but also that losing her had broken him.

Alec: Go get some sleep so that you're fresh for your first full day with your daughter. She's one hell of a kid, by the way.

His brother signed off, and Harry took Alec's advice, closing the laptop and getting under the covers.

And despite the nearly inconceivable stress of the day, thinking of Amelia had him smiling as he fell asleep.

CHAPTER SEVEN

The next morning, when Molly rolled over and looked at the bedside clock, she was shocked to see that it was nine a.m.

Since the day she'd given birth to Amelia, she hadn't slept past six thirty. Her daughter was a naturally early riser, so Molly had to adapt her night-owl tendencies to hers.

Could there be a worse morning to sleep in? She should have been there when Amelia woke up in a strange bed, should have been beside her for every second of her first morning with Harry. Not snoring away in his ridiculously comfortable guest bed.

Molly leaped out of the bed, threw on her clothes from the night before, and ran out of the room and down the hall, taking the stairs two at a time.

Only to skid to a halt when she saw them.

Amelia and Harry were sitting at the kitchen island laughing together, their heads thrown back, looking like two peas in a pod. Aldwin leaned against Amelia's legs while she stroked his ruff. The kitchen was a mess of pots and pans, and their plates looked as though they'd licked them clean.

It made Molly's heart swell to watch them. Though they'd met only yesterday, she could see that Harry already cared deeply for Amelia and wanted to make this transition as easy as possible for her. It was a huge relief to know that he wouldn't keep her at the same distance that he had kept Molly.

That was, she had to remind herself, *if* it turned out that Harry was definitely Amelia's father.

Molly realized she had never wanted anything so much in all her life.

That wasn't all she wanted, though. She wanted to be laughing with them, wanted to be part of the bond they were building. Instead, she made herself go back to her room to take a shower and change. She didn't plan on trying to impress Harry. But that didn't mean she needed to walk around looking like the bride of Frankenstein either, especially on such an important day.

Thankfully, she'd had a good night's sleep. As soon as she'd lain down, Harry's voice had started playing in a loop inside her head. *Don't you know it broke me to lose you? The love of my life.* But amazingly, his voice had finally lulled her to sleep.

She couldn't let herself focus on what he'd said about her. She needed to keep every ounce of her focus on making sure Amelia was okay with all these huge changes. Maybe one day in the future, once everything had been worked out...

No. Letting her head, her heart, go down that road was utter madness.

The guest bathroom was as luxurious as the rest of Harry's house, top of the line without being cold or cookie-cutter. After so many years of squeezing into her little corner shower, with barely enough room to lift her legs to shave them, it was such a pleasure to stand beneath the dual sprays. As she toweled off a few minutes later, she was surprised to look in the mirror and see that instead of looking like she'd just been run over by an emotional train, her eyes were bright, her skin was flushed, and even her lips seemed fuller.

This was what being around Harry did to her. Made normal and simple seem extraordinary and special. She'd always felt prettier, smarter, more adventurous when they were together.

Deliberately, she turned away from the mirror. The very last thing she needed was to go all gooey and breathless over Harry again. What they'd shared had been a long time ago. They were both different people now.

She, for one, was stronger. As a single mother completely on her own, she'd had to be.

As for Harry? Well, she wasn't sure yet how he'd

changed. Except to become hugely successful...and even better looking.

Seriously, she thought as she reached into her bag for clean clothes, then dressed and finger-combed her wet hair, she needed to get over her reaction to him— the sparks that exploded through her every time he got close—before she went downstairs. Once they confirmed that he was Amelia's father, he was going to be her co-parent. Nothing more.

Even if he'd said it had broken him to lose her...then called her the love of his life. All after she had confessed that she'd longed for Amelia to be his all along.

"Mom!" Amelia spotted her first as she walked into the kitchen a few minutes later.

"Oh, honey." Molly threw her arms around the person who meant absolutely everything to her. "I'm so glad you're okay. I love you so much." She didn't ever want to let go, but when Amelia made a sound as though Molly was squashing all the oxygen out of her, she pulled back a little bit. "Don't you ever do something like that again."

"I won't." But the truth was that her daughter didn't look all that apologetic. "How could you not tell me about him, Mom?" Two spots of color bloomed on Amelia's cheeks. She was clearly upset as she said, "I always figured my dad must be a horrible person. But

Harry is the best!"

Though Molly hated it when Amelia was mad at her, she was glad she'd immediately asked the difficult question—always so brave, even now, when everything had gone completely topsy-turvy.

Molly sent a quick questioning glance at Harry, and he nodded to let her know he was on board with getting right to it.

Without letting go of Amelia's hands, though Harry's dog was doing his best to claim her all for himself again, Molly said, "I know you must be furious with me for keeping Harry from you for your whole life—and I don't blame you for feeling that way—but I swear I had no idea that he was actually your father."

"What do you mean?" Amelia frowned. "How could you not know? Harry was your boyfriend."

"He was, but we broke up toward the end of our freshman year. And then…" God, this was hard. "After we broke up, there was someone else." Molly licked her lips, as uncomfortable as she'd ever been, though she'd always tried to speak frankly with Amelia about sex and boys. "I was only with the other guy once, and I broke the one big rule. I had unprotected sex with him. When I found out I was pregnant, based on lots of factors, I was sure you had to be his, not Harry's. And I'm afraid you were right—that other guy wasn't a nice person, honey. Not at all."

Amelia didn't look particularly shocked by her mother's one-night-stand confession. At fifteen, she'd surely heard a million times worse on the Internet. But she did look confused—and more than a little panicked. "So if everything happened just like you said, then how could I have a DNA test that says I'm Harry's?"

"That's what I was wondering when he called yesterday. I didn't see how it could be possible. Until Harry told me his aunt had gotten her period in the first month of one of her pregnancies, and she didn't realize she was pregnant. I never knew that could happen, and my obstetrician never mentioned it as a possibility. But I found a bunch of articles about it on my phone last night before I went to bed—so now I know it's definitely possible. If you want to read any of them, I can show them to you."

"All I want is to know for sure that Harry is my dad."

"We all want that," Harry agreed.

Molly appreciated that he had let her explain things to Amelia by herself before stepping into the conversation, but she also understood that from here on out, they needed to be equal partners with her, which was why she let him take over from there.

"We're going to get another DNA test," he said. "And then none of us will ever have to doubt again that you're my daughter."

"Can we go right now?" Amelia asked, intent on putting any uncertainty behind her.

"The doctor said to come by as soon as we're ready." Harry turned to Molly. "Do you want some breakfast first?"

She shook her head. "Let's go."

★ ★ ★

The friendly and efficient doctor, who was a friend of Alec's, had said he'd be happy to expedite the test. Within a matter of minutes, Amelia's and Harry's blood had been taken and sent off to the lab. They were told to expect the results within the hour, and soon the three of them were out standing on the sidewalk.

Though Molly was riddled with anxiety over the test results, the nerves on Amelia's face made her want to do whatever she could to make the waiting go faster. "Do you remember that carousel we rode on one of our dates, Harry?" Her chest ached at the bittersweet memory. She wasn't sure that reenacting something from their past was a good idea. But being a mother was about putting her child first, no matter what. "Isn't it just around the corner?"

At first, Harry looked at her like she was crazy to bring up one of their old dates now. But she soon saw understanding dawn.

"Sure is." His voice sounded a little too hearty and overly excited about a carousel ride they'd taken in college, but at least he was trying.

"What do you say the three of us ride it while we wait?" Molly put her arm around her daughter's waist. "It's this way. And if I'm remembering correctly, we went to an ice cream shop afterward." She made herself smile at Harry, even as she was suddenly hit with an extremely potent memory of him licking a drop of her strawberry ice cream from her lips.

It was amazing how quickly the memories came flooding back when she wasn't shoving them all away, the way she'd been doing ever since their breakup.

* * *

If Harry had been asked to predict the likelihood of ever riding Jane's Carousel in Brooklyn with Molly again, he would have said there was a greater chance of aliens landing in the middle of Central Park. *Much* greater.

"I can't believe you guys went on a date here," Amelia said. "It's like stepping back in time."

"It wasn't *that* long ago," Molly said.

"You probably wore bell bottoms and flowers in your hair," Amelia teased.

When Molly laughed with Amelia, Harry's heart swelled inside his chest. So big that he was surprised his

lungs could contain it. It was nearly killing him, waiting
to hear from the doctor, but Molly was a genius for
having them come here to take their minds off the
ticking clock. Especially now that Amelia had found
her smile again.

"The only thing missing is Aldwin," Amelia said. "I
miss him already."

The dog had whined so loudly when Amelia
walked out the front door that morning that she'd run
back inside to pet him and promise him they wouldn't
be long.

"He'll be okay for a couple of hours," Harry assured her, "although I'm thinking he's probably going
to stick to you like glue the next time you try to leave."

"I wish he could go back to A Bay with me," Amelia said.

Harry's heart hurt at the thought of Amelia being
five hours away. There were so many things they were
going to need to figure out once the DNA test came
back positive. *It damn well better come back positive!* But it
was hard to think clearly about the details of their daily
lives when he was still just trying to take in the basics.

During the drive to the doctor's office, Harry had
learned Amelia's favorite color—teal. Her favorite
food—Thai summer rolls. Her favorite book—*Wonder*.
Her favorite TV show—*Friends*. He'd been surprised
that she was familiar with an old show, but evidently

she and Molly had binge-watched all ten seasons together.

Harry had never been much for TV, but now he desperately wanted to binge-watch something with his daughter. Just spend hour upon hour sitting together on the couch eating summer rolls beneath a teal blanket. He almost had to laugh at himself, the vision was so clear.

"I read some stuff about you on the Internet when I was on the bus here," Amelia said as the carousel went 'round and 'round. "Did you really discover all that new stuff about medieval battles?"

"I didn't exactly discover it. I just took the data and put it together in a different way than anyone else had so far."

"Harry is being modest," Molly said. "He's the smartest person I've ever met, apart from you, honey."

If I'm so smart, he wanted to ask, *then how could I have gotten everything so wrong with you?*

Even now, he couldn't keep from staring at her while she rode her giraffe, her hair blowing in the breeze, her skin flushed. Nothing had changed since the first time he'd set eyes on her in the library—she was still the only woman who made him feel something way down deep inside. Something young, and wild, and oh so sweet.

"Are you working on another groundbreaking project now?" Amelia asked.

"I'm halfway through my new book, but I'm not sure when it's going to be done. I've been blocked on it for a while."

"Sometimes I get blocked while I'm working on a paper," Amelia commiserated. "Mom is really good at helping me through it. Maybe she can help you too."

"You know what, I think you're on to something." He looked at Molly. Maybe she would be wary about helping with his book, but if the test was positive, then they were going to be seeing a lot of each other in the future. "Any chance I could interest you in reading a really rough draft of my book? The half that's done, anyway."

Molly's cheeks were more flushed than ever as she said, "I'm sure there's someone with better qualifications who could help. Besides, I don't have my degree yet."

He was on the verge of asking why, when he realized he already knew. Molly had been a single mother, responsible for absolutely everything when it came to Amelia. And she'd told him that she always put her daughter first. Even, it seemed, when it meant taking nearly two decades to earn her degree.

"Now that I'm in high school, Mom is really cruising on it," Amelia said, proud of her mother. "She's always studying. And sometimes she even asks for *my* help with her homework."

"That's because you always see the things I don't," Molly said with a smile.

Harry turned to Amelia. "It sounds like I should ask you to read my book too."

"Really?" Amelia looked as though he'd just asked her to go to a music festival, as opposed to slogging through a painfully rough draft of his book.

"Really."

"Cool, I'd love to tell you what I think."

The two of them grinned at each other, and even with the test results still hanging over them, Harry couldn't remember the last time he'd felt this happy.

But that wasn't true. He knew exactly when he'd last felt this way: Whenever he and Molly had been together, talking or studying or laughing or making love. Every moment he'd been able to steal away with her had been precious.

Just then, the teenager managing the carousel announced that their turn was ending and they'd have to disembark.

"Now we go get ice cream, right?" Amelia said once they were back outside. "Mom, I'll bet you got strawberry on your date, didn't you?" When Molly nodded, Amelia turned to Harry. "What flavor did you get?"

He couldn't remember, only that he'd licked the

strawberry ice cream from Molly's lips.

Into the silence, Molly said, barely above a whisper, "Rocky Road."

"I love that flavor too!" Amelia exclaimed.

Harry relished Amelia's easy affection, her bright spirit. She was so much like his sister and his female cousins. Though she hadn't been raised around them, she would fit right in with the rest of the family.

"We're so much alike," she continued. "I knew we would be."

She hooked one of her arms through his, the other through Molly's, and as they walked down the street, he caught sight of the three of them in a store window. They looked like a happy family, out enjoying a sunny day in Brooklyn.

A family that had taken fifteen years to come together.

A family still waiting to find out if they really *were* a family.

"How cute is this place?" Amelia said. They got in line at the end of a good two dozen people waiting to order, and that was when Harry's phone rang.

All of them looked at his pocket.

"Oh God..." Molly was pale as she reached for Amelia's hand.

With a shaking hand, Harry pulled out his phone. He'd stopped breathing by the time he answered and put the phone to his ear, and there was so much blood rushing into his head that he almost couldn't hear what the doctor said.

"Say it again," he said into the phone, his voice so full of emotion the words came out all garbled up.

The second time, he knew he'd heard right.

"Thank you." He hung up and put the phone in his pocket. "You're mine, Amelia. I'm your father."

She threw her arms around him, and then Molly was in there too—all three of them hugging each other tightly, laughing and crying together.

CHAPTER EIGHT

Amelia pulled out her phone. "Mom, Harry—" She grinned like a Cheshire cat. "I mean, *Dad*, come be in the picture with me."

Amelia took the picture, and he caught a quick flash of it before she moved the phone away—the image of a fifteen-year-old girl glowing with happiness between her father, who looked like every dream he'd ever had had just come true, and her mother, who looked slightly stunned, as though she wasn't exactly sure how any of this had happened.

Amelia's fingers flew over her phone's screen. "People are going to *freak* when they see this picture."

"You didn't just put it up on Instagram, did you?" Molly asked, even though she had already pulled out her phone to look. She read the caption out loud. *"First ever pic with my mom AND dad! #familygoals."* Molly lifted wide eyes to their daughter. "You just told everyone who follows you about Harry, and you tagged me so everyone who follows me will also see it! I thought we were all going to sit down to figure out how we want to tell everyone the big news."

"No way. I waited fifteen years for this—I'm telling *everyone* as fast as I can." To illustrate her point, she turned to one of the people in line behind them. "This is my dad. Isn't he awesome?"

Though the woman looked a little bemused, she smiled and said, "He looks very nice."

"Dad, what's your Instagram name?" Amelia asked. "I want to tag you too."

Harry was finding it hard to speak around the lump in his throat at hearing her call him *Dad*. It was a word he'd never tire of hearing. "*@HarrisonJackSullivan.*"

"Is the Jack after someone special?" she asked as she quickly added his tag to her post.

"My father was really close to his brother Jack."

"Cool. I can't wait to meet Great Uncle Jack."

"He passed away when I was a kid, unfortunately. But his wife, Mary, the one your mom told you about this morning, is one of the greatest people you'll ever meet. Her eight kids are also amazing. They're all out in Northern California."

"I've never been to California," Amelia said. "Never been on a plane, actually. But we've driven to Vermont, Massachusetts, Connecticut, Rhode Island— and of course Canada, because we're spitting distance from Kingston." Without so much as pausing to take a breath, she asked, "For my next school break, can we go to California to see Aunt Mary and your cousins and their families?"

Harry wanted to say yes to every single thing Amelia asked for. But Molly was still looking a little shell-shocked. By the way she'd hugged him after the doctor had given them the test results, he knew she was happy that he was definitely Amelia's father. But it also meant plenty of big changes on tap for the three of them. No matter how much he and Molly wanted to keep things on an even keel for Amelia, the truth was that nothing would be the same as before.

"We've got plenty of time to figure all of that out," he told Amelia.

"Are you sure?" Amelia looked panicked again. "I don't want to have to leave tonight to go back to school tomorrow and then only see you on weekends or school breaks. How are we going to see each other when you live and work here?"

Suddenly, what he needed to do was obvious. "I'm going to take a leave of absence."

"You are?" Molly looked doubly shell-shocked now.

He nodded. It was exactly the right decision.

Nothing was more important than his newfound daughter. And even before Amelia had rung his doorbell, he'd been thinking about Molly. Wanting to search for her, wanting to find her, wanting to see if it was possible for them to have a second chance at love.

This was it, he realized with sudden clarity. Not only his chance to be a father, but also his chance to love Molly the way she deserved to be loved. With all of his heart, instead of merely the leftover parts of it.

No matter what, he vowed to get things right from here on out.

With Amelia *and* Molly.

"I'll call the dean right now to let her know my plans," he said, "and then I'll head to Alexandria Bay with you both tonight."

"Yay!" Amelia threw her arms around him and hugged him tight.

But Molly didn't jump into the hug with them this time. "Harry, we should really talk about this before you make any plans."

"Sure," he said, though it was only for Amelia's benefit. "If you get to the front of the line while we're talking—" He handed Amelia a twenty. "—get my scoop in a waffle cone."

Though he and Molly walked far enough away that Amelia wouldn't hear them, they stayed close enough to keep an eye on her.

"Are you sure this is a good idea?" Molly asked him.

"I don't see how spending time with Amelia could ever be a bad idea."

And you, he thought. *I want to spend time with you. All the time I missed when I was too young and stupid not to take you for granted. All the time we should have spent together to see if we could have made it, not just as college sweethearts, but for the long haul.*

But he knew better than to say any of that to her this soon, just minutes after they'd gotten the results of the second DNA test.

They needed to get through one big change at time. First, Amelia finding him and Harry learning he was her father. Then, Harry moving to Alexandria Bay. And after that?

He'd never hoped for more, never wanted anything as much as he wanted to share his heart with his daughter—and with Molly too.

"Of course I want you to spend time with Amelia," Molly was saying, "but what are you going to do in our little town during the hours when she's at school and practicing for her musical and hanging out with her friends?"

"I'm sure I can find plenty of ways to entertain myself."

Molly's skin flushed, as though she was imagining all the ways they used to entertain each other. "I'm sure you can," she said in a slightly husky voice. "Well, if you think the university will be okay with you leaving on such short notice, then you're right—

Amelia will love having you close by while still being able to live her normal life at school and with her friends."

As Harry went to call the dean, he hoped Molly would love having him close by too.

* * *

Perhaps Molly should have found it hard to imagine Harry in Alexandria Bay.

But it was all too easy.

Another man with his legacy of fame and wealth would surely wear it like a crown wherever he went. But Harry had always fit easily into every situation, every group, every room. A born mediator, a middle child, he knew exactly what to say and do, not only to keep from pushing people's buttons, but also to make them happy.

Although the way he'd been looking at her when he'd been pressing his case for coming to Alexandria Bay—with heat in his eyes, the way he used to right before he kissed her and stripped away her clothes— had made her breath hitch in her chest.

Surely she was imagining that heat. After all, the past twenty-four hours had them all reeling.

While Harry called the dean of the history department, Molly rejoined Amelia in line.

"He's definitely going to come to A Bay, isn't he?"

Amelia asked.

"I don't think there's anything on the planet that could keep him from coming."

"When I got to his house last night," Amelia said, "I didn't know if he'd believe I was his, or want to talk to me. But not only was he totally great about everything, now he's going to be just down the hall."

"Down the hall?" Molly had to have heard Amelia wrong. "Harry isn't going to *stay* with us."

"Why not? We have an extra bedroom."

There were so many reasons *why not* that Molly didn't know where to start. Most of them began and ended with the fact that every time she looked at him, she either drooled or heated up all over. And now she was even imagining that he was looking at her with desire.

Darn it, she was supposed to have gotten over this before she came down to the kitchen this morning. Clearly, she had a heck of a lot of work to do keeping her hormones from raging out of control whenever Harry was near. It had been bad enough being together last night and this morning in Harry's large home. Inside her tiny little cottage, there would be no way for either of them to keep a safe distance from each other.

"I'm sure we can find him a rental really close by," Molly suggested.

"But I want to have breakfast with my dad every

morning," Amelia protested. "When I come home after school, I want him to be there, not on the other side of town. And if I have questions about homework, I want to be able to ask them without calling him on the phone. Or if I'm watching a show, I want him to be able to watch it with me." Amelia's eyes bored into Molly's. "I didn't get to be with my dad for fifteen years. Now that I've finally found him, shouldn't I get to be with him as much as possible?"

"Are you two going to order, or not?"

They both turned to look at the irritated server, but Molly was too flattened by the look on Amelia's face when she'd said, *I didn't get to be with my dad for fifteen years*, to respond.

Amelia took over the ordering. "Can we get two waffle cones with a scoop of Rocky Road and a scoop of strawberry in a cup?"

Molly was still reeling—from the DNA test *and* the thought of Harry moving in with them—when she and Amelia headed outside with the ice cream.

"Do you think he still loves you? Do you still love him?"

Molly nearly dropped her ice cream, barely managing not to sputter as she said, "We haven't seen each other in nearly sixteen years."

"Yeah, but obviously you loved each other enough back in college to have me. He doesn't seem to be with anyone. And you've never dated any guy you really liked."

Before Molly could figure out her reply, Harry came over and took his cone from Amelia.

"Everything's set. My classes will be covered by my head TA. I just need to drop by my office to pick up a couple of things after we're done with our ice cream." He grinned at Amelia. "I'm really looking forward to seeing your house and school and meeting your friends."

"It's going to be amazing," Amelia agreed. "Especially with you staying with us."

Harry's eyebrows went up. "Molly?" He turned to look at her in surprise. "You and Amelia want me to stay with you?"

Despite her reservations, Molly wanted to do whatever she could to help Amelia get to know her father. And she was also desperate to make it up to Harry for her massive mistake. "We both think it would be better that way, as opposed to you getting a rental in town."

"This way we can be close to each other all the time," Amelia said. "And Aldwin too."

Molly barely stifled a groan. How could she have forgotten Harry's dog? Yes, he was sweet, but he was also huge. And her cottage was tiny.

"Will you do it?" Amelia asked Harry. "Will you

and Aldwin stay with us?"

He grinned at Amelia. "Aldwin and I would be very happy to accept your invitation to stay in your home."

★ ★ ★

Molly hadn't been back on the Columbia University campus since freshman year. "It looks the same and yet totally different." She looked at a twentysomething girl coming down the steps. "Probably because I feel about a hundred years older."

Harry laughed, and the sound vibrated all the way through her. Especially her foolish heart that should know better. "I know what you mean. When I started teaching, though I was barely older than the students, it already felt like there was a massive age difference between us."

They walked inside the building and down the hall to Harry's office. Lost in the past, Molly found herself saying, "I'd love to see one of your lectures. I've read some of your work online, but I'm sure you really bring medieval history to life in your classes."

He had just unlocked his office door and was about to step inside when he turned back to her. "You've read my work?"

She didn't realize he had stopped in his tracks until she nearly plowed into him. Amelia didn't stop fast enough, however, and *did* plow into Molly—which meant Molly stumbled into Harry's chest. His arms automatically went around her and Amelia to steady them both, with Molly as the filling to their sandwich.

In an instant, she catalogued half a dozen things about Harry: his taut muscles, the searing heat of his body, the way his pupils dilated when he looked into her eyes, the fact that his delicious clean, masculine scent hadn't changed.

But most of all...how much she wanted him.

More than ever before.

And that was saying something, considering how insatiable she'd been for him way back when.

"Are you okay?" His voice was slightly hoarse, as though he was feeling the same things.

No, she couldn't let herself go there. Couldn't let herself dream of being with him again. Not when so much had already changed in their lives.

Besides, for all she knew, he was with someone else. A woman as brilliant and charismatic and well connected as he. Someone he would trust with his whole heart, instead of just tiny pieces of it. Someone he would ask to help him when he needed it. Someone he would want on his team, instead of always feeling that he had to soldier on alone.

Molly made herself shift away from him, pushing Amelia back with her hip so that she could move to a safer place. Anywhere Harry wasn't touching her. He led them into his office.

"I'm fine," she finally said, even though she was nearly as far from *fine* as she'd ever been. "Like I said this morning, though I wasn't able to finish my degree here, I wanted to continue my studies in any way I could. Since you're one of the top minds in the field, it made sense to read your work."

"I can't believe you had to leave school when you got pregnant with me," Amelia said. "It's not like it was the Middle Ages, or anything."

"Well, the school didn't kick me out." Molly felt horribly put on the spot. It was a sensation she should have been used to after the past twenty-four hours. Clearly, she was a slow learner. "But like I said, the guy I thought was your dad wasn't very nice. I needed to make sure he wouldn't try to take you away from me, which is why I left."

Amelia turned to Harry. "If Mom had thought you were my father and told you about me, wouldn't you have helped?"

"Of course I would have."

"I wish I had gotten to know you before now," Amelia said in a shaky voice. "I wish I had grown up with you as my dad. Instead of always wondering. And instead of Mom thinking some total creep was my father."

"I do too," Harry said, emotion making his words

sound thick, heavy.

"You know what's weird?" Amelia flopped onto his couch. "Your office is almost exactly like the archive room at Boldt Castle. Full of a ton of books and maps and a big desk and a leather seat."

Harry looked momentarily surprised by her *non sequitur*. If Molly's heart hadn't currently been in her throat, she might have laughed. He was quickly learning the way a fifteen-year-old's mind worked, jumping from one subject to another totally unrelated one without pause. Right when you thought you were having a heart-to-heart, your teenager would start talking about fixing a chip in her nail polish.

"Speaking of castles," Harry said as he walked over to his desk, "what kind of work do you do at Boldt Castle?"

Molly had to work really hard not to notice what a seriously hot professor he was. She could only imagine the way his students must drool over him. Especially if he put on the reading glasses on his desk. *Swoon.* Of course, she doubted he noticed his students' reactions to him. Harry would never consider having a relationship with someone he was teaching.

"I work in the gift shop." From the start, Molly's boss had been so nice that if her babysitter ever fell through, she had been allowed to bring Amelia to work with her.

"She doesn't just work there," Amelia said. "She manages the whole place. She redid their inventory system and is putting in a new ticket system online. But she loves the historical archives most of all, don't you, Mom?"

"I do." Molly smiled at her daughter. Amelia had always been her biggest champion. "Every time I'm in there, I learn something new."

"You guys must have been total nerds when you were together," Amelia commented as she grabbed one of the leather-bound books on a side table and started flipping through it.

"I don't know if we were nerds *all* the time." Harry's words held enough warmth that Molly couldn't help but be thrown into vivid memories of the deliciously un-nerdy things they'd done together. "Although we did meet in the library."

Amelia looked between the two of them thoughtfully. Then she smiled.

Molly wasn't stupid. She could guess at the direction Amelia's mind was spinning. Especially after her questions about whether Harry might still love Molly, and if Molly might still love him back. If it was great to finally have her father in her life, surely Amelia would think it would be even better to get her parents back together.

But though the situation might seem clear-cut to a

fifteen-year-old, in reality Molly and Harry's relationship was anything but clear. Even when they were
dating, she'd never really known where she stood. And
now?

Now, she had so much to make up to both Harry
and Amelia. Time they could never get back. Memories they would never have.

Thankfully, Harry didn't seem to have noticed the
matchmaking gleam in Amelia's eyes as he unplugged
his laptop and slid it into a leather bag, then gathered
up several stacks of papers and put them in with his
computer, and his glasses.

Molly silently prayed he would never put those on
in front of her. Otherwise, it just might be her undoing.

Harry gave his desk and shelves one last scan.
"That should do it."

A knock came at the open door, and then a guy
looked in. With the requisite man bun, beard, and
cuffed jeans, Molly guessed he was in his mid to late
twenties. "Professor Sullivan, sorry to intrude. I
thought I heard voices and figured I'd check to see if
you were in."

"Amelia, Molly, this is my teaching assistant, Kelsin," Harry said. He looked so proud as he said,
"Amelia is my daughter."

Kelsin shook her hand. "It's great to meet you,
Amelia. Your dad is a superstar."

"I know." Amelia looked as though she might burst with joy over being related to Harry.

Kelsin shook Molly's hand next, holding on a little too long, while staring into her eyes with enough intensity that she wondered if she reminded him of someone. His mother maybe?

"Are you new to the department, Molly?" Kelsin asked. "I'm sure I would remember if we had met before."

"No, I'm not. I used to be a student here, though, about a million years ago."

Kelsin gave her a charming smile. "It couldn't have been that long," he said in a smooth voice.

"What do you need, Kelsin?" Harry's voice boomed into their conversation, which was when Molly realized he had come to stand next to her. Really close. And he was glowering.

It was a look very few people ever saw on Harry Sullivan.

Kelsin looked between the two of them, then at Amelia. Finally, he must have pieced *Mom + Dad = Teenager* together.

He lifted his hands slightly as he took a step back. "I just got a text from Dean McIntyre saying that you're going on a leave of absence. Are you sure you're okay with me taking over your classes?"

"It's fine," Harry growled, rather than thanking his

assistant for the help.

"Cool." Kelsin took another step toward the door. "Then I'll get out of your hair and email if I have any questions."

"Fine," Harry said again and closed the door behind him with a bang.

The door had barely shut when Amelia said, "Mom, he was totally flirting with you!"

"He wasn't."

"He was." Harry didn't look at all happy about it either.

"Guys flirt with her all the time," Amelia told him.

Molly nearly groaned at how obvious Amelia was being. She'd have to nip this matchmaking idea in the bud, pronto.

Harry slung his leather bag over his shoulder, then yanked open his door so hard it nearly came off the hinges. "I'm done here. We can head back to my place to pack up."

Okay, so Harry *did* seem a tad jealous. But Molly knew he was probably only reacting to someone flirting with her because they'd once been together. Jealousy was surely nothing more than some remembered instinct.

Harry had always been a little on the possessive side, she thought with a little shiver. In the *best* kind of way...

God, she really needed to stop thinking back to those nights when they'd barely make it inside her dorm room before he'd rip off her clothes and take her. But, oh, it was so hard to push away such sweetly sinful memories. And only getting harder with every second they spent together.

How was she going to handle having Harry in her house?

Molly honestly had no idea.

CHAPTER NINE

While Harry packed, Amelia and Molly made sandwiches for the road. From his bedroom upstairs, Harry could hear Amelia praising Aldwin for being a good boy. No doubt the dog was making out like a bandit with the lunch meat. Aldwin knew a soft touch when he saw one. Two soft touches—Molly loved animals as much as their daughter.

First thing that morning, Harry had sent a text to Drake, Suzanne, Alec, and his father to let them know that he'd fill them in on everything shortly. He hadn't told any of them last night about Molly's doubts over his paternity, which meant they didn't yet know about the second DNA test. Thankfully, they'd understood from his short text that he needed some time alone with Amelia and Molly without his phone going off like crazy. But when he heard Suzanne's ringtone coming from his pocket, he knew the timer on his sister's patience was up. Honestly, she'd made it a good hour longer than he'd expected.

"Amelia is doing great," he said as soon as he

picked up, easily anticipating her first question.

"Oh good. She's adorable, and I want to talk to her before we hang up. Now, how are you? And is Molly there?"

"Yes, Molly's here. And I'm good." Amelia's laughter and Aldwin's answering bark made him smile. "Best I've ever been, actually."

"I'm so glad," Suzanne said. "I was worried about how things would go between you and Molly last night after we left. Alec said you weren't mad at her for some reason, but I've got to confess that I don't understand how you couldn't be."

This was a conversation he'd better get used to having. Not only with his family, but also with friends who would want to know how on earth neither he nor Molly had known he was Amelia's father.

"After we broke up, she was absolutely certain she couldn't be pregnant," he explained. "And from the details she gave me, I can understand why she thought that. It wasn't until she dated someone else that she realized she was, in fact, pregnant. So of course she assumed the other guy was Amelia's father. Even her doctor agreed that the dates lined up. It never occurred to anyone back then that the early months of her pregnancy were anything but normal—or that I could be Amelia's father. Remember how Aunt Mary didn't know she was pregnant with the twins at first? The same thing happened with Molly."

"But if all that's true," Suzanne said slowly, "then are you absolutely sure the other guy *isn't* the father? I know Amelia did that online DNA test, but—"

"We did another test this morning with Alec's doctor friend in Brooklyn," Harry cut in. "He confirmed that I'm Amelia's dad."

"Thank God." Suzanne gave a loud sigh of relief. "I always really liked Molly, but one day she was there, and the next she wasn't. Remind me, why did you guys break up?"

"It's a long story." One it wouldn't help to dredge up. Especially now that his father was in such a good place. "Suffice it to say, the timing wasn't right for things to work out between us back then."

"But could you work it out now? Especially now that you know you're both Amelia's parents?"

This wasn't the first time Suzanne had read his thoughts. His sister's brain worked so fast and went so deep, that mind-reading actually didn't seem that far outside the realm of possibility. Still, he told her what he'd been reminding himself. "One thing at a time, Suz. I've just given notice to the dean in the history department that I'm taking a leave of absence. I'm packing right now to head to Alexandria Bay this afternoon. They've invited me to stay with them."

If she was at all stunned by this turn of events, she

didn't let on. "Of course you should go to Alexandria Bay to be with them. And staying in their house is perfect. Not only because you and Amelia will really get a chance to know each other that way, but because this will also give you and Molly some good time together to see if you want to rekindle things."

"I wish it was that easy," he admitted, given that Suzanne had already guessed his intentions, even over the phone. "But given how bad Molly feels about everything, I'm not sure it will be. She's thrilled that I'm Amelia's father," he clarified, "and she's an incredible mother, but she's twisting herself up in knots with guilt over not figuring out Amelia's paternity before now, even though it's not her fault." Every time he thought about the way she'd looked when she'd been crying and apologizing in the kitchen, his heart felt like it was going to break.

"It's not your fault either, Harry." His sister knew him well enough to read between the lines of what he hadn't yet said.

"I'm not blameless. Not in the least."

"That still doesn't mean you should beat yourself up for a past you can't go back and change. We've seen Dad do that his whole life. I couldn't stand to see you do that too. None of us could."

Despite the emotions roiling through him, he couldn't deny that what Suzanne was saying made sense. Harry and his siblings knew better than anyone that you couldn't go back and change the past—and just how much continually mourning the past and the mistakes you made could destroy the present. The last thing he wanted to do was to let past hurts and resentments harm his new, growing bond with Amelia.

What if he and Molly could start fresh too?

"I know it's probably hard to see the forest for the trees right now," Suzanne added, "but at least think about what I'm saying. Otherwise, we're all going to worry about you."

"I will," he promised. "Yesterday was pretty crazy—and you guys came through for me and Amelia big time—but everything's good now. You don't have to worry about me anymore."

"You always say that, Harry, but everyone needs help. Especially with something as huge as learning you're the father of a teenage daughter. You've always taken such good care of us, always helped us when we needed it. Now we're going to do the same for you. And Amelia. And Molly too. Because whether or not you end up getting romantically involved with her again, she's still going to be an important part of our lives from here on out."

Suzanne's offer of support was an almost perfect echo of what Alec had said, only his sister was making it clear that his siblings intended to support all three of them.

"Now, go find Amelia for me," Suzanne said. "I want to talk with her before you hit the road."

Harry headed downstairs to the kitchen, where Amelia was doing some sort of dance in the middle of the room that included a very bemused-looking Aldwin on his hind legs. Molly was laughing so hard she was clutching her stomach.

"Amelia, your Aunt Suzanne is on the phone. She wants to say hi."

Amelia stopped dancing with Aldwin, then grabbed the phone from Harry's hand. "Aunt Suzanne!" Amelia nodded vigorously at whatever Harry's sister said. "It's the best news ever, right? And now he's coming to stay with us for a while too!"

Harry joined Molly at the kitchen island, where she was cleaning up after having made sandwiches.

"Everyone at school is freaking out and can't wait to meet my dad," Amelia said into the phone. "I've told them about all of you too, so hopefully you can come up soon. Actually..." She bit her lip, looking slightly uncertain. "I'm going to be in *The Sound of Music* on Friday. I'm Louisa, the one who's always reading a book. I know it's a long way to come—"

Though Harry couldn't make out what his sister said, her reply was obvious when Amelia's grin threatened to split her face.

"Seriously? That would be amazing if you were able to come! Especially because Friday is also my mom's birthday, so you could be there for that too."

Molly shot Harry a look, one that grew more and more panicked as Amelia continued speaking. Of course he remembered Friday was Molly's birthday. How could he forget when it was also the anniversary of his mother's death?

"We don't have a ton of room at our house," Amelia went on, "especially now that Dad's going to be in the guest room, but we could find sleeping bags." She paused to let Suzanne respond, then said, "Yeah, there's a hotel close to our house. That will totally work."

As Amelia and Suzanne chatted, it became clear that their conversation wasn't going to end anytime soon. Harry said to Molly, "Are you okay with my family coming on Friday? Suzanne just said she wanted to chat with Amelia. I didn't realize she was going to round up the whole gang for a road trip to Alexandria Bay."

"I think it's amazing that your family are all so thrilled to be a part of Amelia's life. She's a part of your family now, a big family too, which is what I know she's always wanted. I would never get in the way of that."

"But you're still concerned about something, aren't

you?"

She bit her lip, looking so much like Amelia when she felt uncertain. "I'm nervous," she admitted. "What if your family aren't as forgiving as you've been? If they are angry, it's no less than I deserve."

"Molly." He wanted to reach for her, wanted to take her hands in his, and he might have if Aldwin hadn't shoved his head beneath his hand just then. "I've told Suzanne what happened—what she needs to know, at least. She doesn't judge you or blame you. And after everyone else is filled in, no one else is going to judge you or blame you either."

"I do," she said softly.

He knew exactly how she felt, because he felt the same way about himself. But Suzanne was right—the two of them beating themselves up wasn't going to help anyone. Least of all Amelia.

"We could argue all day about who has more blame to shoulder, but that won't help Amelia, will it?"

"No," she said after a few beats. "I suppose it won't."

"So then, what do you say you and I make a fresh start?"

She looked stunned by his suggestion. "Do you really think that's possible?"

"I hope so." Unable to keep his distance, he moved closer. "The more I think about it, the more I wonder if the best thing we can do is look forward, rather than staying focused on the past."

Molly cocked her head. "Isn't that pretty much the exact opposite of what a history professor should say? Aren't we supposed to learn from the past so we don't make the same mistakes again?"

"Of course we should learn from our mistakes. But you and I both know that history is rarely clear-cut or straightforward. It can be easy to paint things in black and white, right and wrong. But people are rarely totally good or bad. Mostly, we're all just trying to make the best decisions we can, with the information we have at hand. We don't always get it right." Harry shook his head. "I know I certainly haven't. Which is why I hope you'll give me a second chance. At the very least, to celebrate your birthday with you on Friday…and to get it right this time."

Now she looked even *more* stunned. "I know what a big day it is for your family, Harry. Especially your father."

"He's doing a lot better this year." Harry silently prayed his father's outlook would keep improving. "And since it sounds like my family is coming for Amelia's show, there will be plenty of people there to support him if he needs it."

Before she could respond, Aldwin shoved his head even harder against Harry's hand.

"I'm sorry," Harry said, "Aldwin has obviously waited until the last second to ask to go out, so I need to take him. But though I know all of this has happened really quickly and unexpectedly, I hope you'll think about what I've said."

* * *

A fresh start.

Only someone as selfless and giving and wonderful as Harry could suggest that.

Molly wanted to leap at his offer.

She also wanted to leap into his arms and never let go.

But could she?

Or would the past haunt them no matter their intentions not to let it?

Especially with Friday looming only a few days away. Not only her birthday, but also the anniversary of the day when Harry had lost his mother. She couldn't imagine how the day was going to play out, other than to know how happy and joyful Amelia would be over the Sullivans coming to see her high school musical.

From the backyard, Harry turned and caught Molly's eye. She couldn't look away, couldn't stop herself from drinking him in. And now, despite her worries about the future, she couldn't hold back a smile.

Just as it always had, simply having him close again was enough to make her heart sing.

* * *

Suzanne Sullivan passed around the plate of cheese and crackers she'd put together for the family meeting. She wasn't much of a cook, and Roman was with a client, so it was the best everyone was going to get. After leaving Harry's house last night, Suzanne, Drake, Alec, and her father had agreed to reconvene at her place this afternoon to discuss Harry's situation—and to decide how to help him, if necessary.

She had just finished relaying the details of her phone call with Harry, when her father said, "Someone remind me, when did Harry and Molly break up?"

"I was a sophomore in high school." Drake hesitated slightly. "The last time she ever called, she sounded upset. I think Harry was supposed to get together with her. But he was at the lake." Drake looked uncomfortable as he said, "I'm pretty sure it was the anniversary of Mom's death."

Suzanne frowned as the pieces started falling into place. "Amelia just told me Molly's birthday is this Friday. The same day that Mom died."

Alec cursed, even as Drake shook his head and said, "You guys don't think that's why they broke up, do you? Because Harry wasn't able to be there for her?"

"It must be." William Sullivan looked gutted. "The year you were a sophomore in high school, Drake, was particularly rough for me. I have no doubt it's my fault that they broke up."

"Dad, wait—" Suzanne began, but William held up a hand to stop her protests.

"Things are still pretty hazy when I look back, but the one thing I do remember with perfect clarity was that Harry was constantly there for me. I must have known he was giving up his own life for my sake, but I was too busy feeling sorry for myself to care. Even though I'd heard him talk about Molly, even though I knew she was important to him, I cared more about myself than about my son."

"Look," Alec said to their father, "I'm not going to absolve you of any of that. But the truth is that you weren't the only one leaning hard on him back then. I was out spending every night at the bars, and he was always coming to get me before I did something really stupid."

Drake nodded. "He was also making sure Suz and I got through high school with good enough grades to get into the universities we wanted."

"Even if he had wanted to make it work with Molly back then," Suzanne said, "how could he?" Her chest hurt thinking about how they'd all taken Harry for granted. "I always wondered why he hasn't yet found anyone."

"He must still have been in love with Molly, all this time," Drake said.

"But he was too busy babysitting us," Alec agreed.

"I've got to make it up to him." Their father stood. "I've got to show him that I don't need to lean on him anymore. And that I'm not going to keep falling apart over your mother."

Suzanne hated seeing her father like this, even if she couldn't argue with what he'd said. "All of us being in Alexandria Bay to support Amelia will be a good start."

"Not good enough." William headed for the door. "I need to buy supplies."

"Supplies?" Drake looked at Suzanne and Alec, then back at William. "For what? A new building project?"

"For a new painting." And then he was out the door and gone.

"Painting?" Suzanne couldn't believe her ears. "Is he serious?"

"He hasn't mentioned anything to me about wanting to paint again," Drake said. "So either this new idea of his is going to be brilliant...or it's going to totally backfire."

"And when it does," Alec said, "Harry's going to feel like he needs to pick up the pieces. Again."

"No." Suzanne was determined. "We can't let that happen. The three of us are officially on Dad duty now. Drake, you figure out what art store Dad's heading to and take the first shift. I'll meet up with him tonight, and then Alec, you've got tomorrow morning. We'll keep rotating through until Friday, at which point we'll all work to keep an eye on him in Alexandria Bay." Her voice softened. "Dad never meant to hurt any of us. Whatever his plan is now, I truly believe he does want to make amends. Even though I know Harry would never hold a grudge or expect anyone to make reparations."

"That's just it," Alec said. "Harry never got angry, never called us out for all we've put him through over the years. We're family, but that's no excuse for not seeing until now all he has given up for us. If not for that, he might never have lost Molly."

"And he wouldn't have missed fifteen years with his daughter either," Drake said.

"He always made sure the three of us were able to go after our dreams. Now it's our turn to make sure he gets his." Suzanne smiled at her brothers. "And I'm pretty sure that those dreams include Amelia *and* Molly."

CHAPTER TEN

The drive to Alexandria Bay clearly wasn't long enough for Aldwin. The wolfhound had never seemed happier than to flop his big furry body across Amelia's lap for five hours straight. Harry had asked her if she was losing the feeling in her legs and needed Aldwin to move to the backseat, but she'd insisted that she and the dog were both right where they needed to be.

Harry knew exactly how Aldwin felt. Five hours with Amelia was an absolutely wonderful gift. They'd talked about everything from her friends to her classes at school to TV and movies—and also about her new family, full of Sullivans who lived all over the world. Alec, Suzanne, and Drake had each texted her during the drive to let her know they would definitely be at her show on Friday night, while her grandfather had called to confirm. From what Harry had been able to tell, it had been a good conversation. So good that as soon as they hung up, Amelia and William continued chatting via text messages.

At first, Harry had been struck by the similarities

between Molly and their daughter—their voices, their expressions, their keen intelligence. But now that he'd spent more time with Amelia, he also saw the ways they were different, unique. Where Molly had always been on the soft-spoken side, Amelia didn't hold anything back. And where Molly rarely asked for anything, Amelia wasn't shy about expressing her wants and desires.

He guessed it was due to their different upbringings. Molly had showered Amelia with love and affection and attention every moment of her life. Whereas Molly's parents had never been there for her.

Harry knew exactly how that felt, how lonely and difficult it could be for a child to find their way without parental guidance. Though his mother had passed away when he was barely older than a toddler, he hadn't only lost her, he'd lost his father, as well, to grief. Harry had never known what it was to have a normal family. To have a mother or father to ask if he needed help with homework after school. To have a dad teach him to ride a bike or throw a ball. To have a parent attend parents' night at school.

He wanted to do all those things for Amelia. But even that didn't feel like it would be enough. He didn't want to simply swoop in and be her long-lost father, while Molly looked on from a distance.

Harry also wanted to be a team with Molly. In every way.

It was amazing how much could change in twenty-four hours. Just one day ago, he'd been a son, a brother, an academic. He'd been wondering where Molly was, what her life was like, whether he should reach out to her.

A day later, he was a *father*.

And Molly was back in his life.

He was grinning as Amelia pointed out the window. "Halfway up the block, that's our cottage."

The sun had nearly set as he parked at the curb. As soon as Amelia clipped on Aldwin's leash, the dog was ready to leap out of the car.

"I'm going to take him for a quick walk down to the corner," Amelia offered. "But don't go inside until I get back. I want to give you the tour myself."

"Okay, but watch out that he doesn't pull you off your feet. He doesn't know his own strength, especially if he sees a squirrel."

"I'll be fine." She smiled at him. "I'm pretty tough. Mom and I took karate lessons at the community center last summer. No one is going to mess with us."

He marveled at Amelia's confidence as the massive wolfhound actually walked at her heel in a way he never had with Harry. Even his kick-ass sister hadn't been this confident when she was fifteen.

Molly pulled into the driveway, and after she'd gotten out of the car, he said, "You've done an amazing job with Amelia."

"Thank you." Molly smiled. "You had a good ride here, I take it?"

"How could I not? Amelia is intelligent and compassionate and funny and kind. And I've never seen Aldwin so tame—or so besotted."

"She has that effect on animals. One look, one word from her, and they all fall at her feet." Molly laughed. "Most people tend to do the same. I've always said she must have been born under a very special star."

Harry wanted to tell Molly that *she* was that star, but he didn't want to scare her off. Not when he was going to be living in her house for the foreseeable future. And not when she still had every reason to be wary of him.

After all, he hadn't exactly apologized for the way he'd broken her heart all those years ago. Hadn't done anything to convince her that he had changed. Sure, he'd taken a leave of absence from his job and temporarily pulled up stakes to spend time with Amelia. But he was so high up the ladder at the university that his career wasn't at all at risk.

Amelia and Aldwin came running down the sidewalk, their long legs eating up the pavement. "I'm ready to give you the tour now," she said, her eyes shining. "This is our front garden. Mom put in the front path and flower beds, but I helped her lay the brick path."

"It looks great." The cottage was yellow, with bright blue trim around the windows. The garden out front echoed the design, the flowers a riot of color all around them.

Amelia headed for the front door, and the second she opened it, Aldwin bounded in. Only to come to a skidding halt in the tiny living room and kitchen.

"I apologize in advance for anything he breaks," Harry said, wondering exactly how three of them and a dog the size of a small horse were going to live here together. The cottage was as warm and welcoming and pretty a home as he'd ever been in. But it was also *tiny*.

"Aldwin's fine," Molly said, giving the dog a pat on his big head as she walked into the kitchen, then put her bag on the counter.

Amelia clearly wasn't the only one excited about having a dog. Growing up in boarding schools while her parents were in far-flung countries, Molly wouldn't have been able to have a pet. He suspected it hadn't been in the cards as a single mother either, not when she'd been so intent on giving every ounce of her attention to her daughter.

"This is our living room and kitchen," Amelia said. "That's Mom's schoolwork on the table." He had already noted the thick textbooks and notebook beside the laptop.

"We don't have an office, but this works just fine," Molly said. "I'll move it all out of the way for dinner."

"I want to make my specialty for Dad's homecoming feast," Amelia said.

Homecoming. That was exactly how it felt, though he'd never been here before.

"Amelia's pasta primavera is to die for," Molly told him.

"After the house tour," Amelia said, "I'll take you out in the garden so we can see what's ripe to go into the dish. I love cooking straight from the garden."

"You're going to love talking food with Alec." Harry couldn't wait for Amelia to spend more time around the rest of his family—he was so glad they would be here on Friday for her musical. "He's recently stepped away from his airplanes to open an organic restaurant in his wife's plant nursery."

"That's so cool," Amelia exclaimed. "Right now, I'm thinking I either want to be a chef or a veterinarian. I used to want to be a lawyer, and then an actor, and then a jewelry maker."

"All great jobs," he said, unable to stop grinning. "Fortunately, you've now got at least one aunt, uncle, or cousin to talk to about pretty much any career you can imagine. Even candy making, like my cousin Cassie in Maine."

"I didn't know you could make an entire career out of candy. She's my hero!" Amelia grabbed his hand to lead him down the hall. "Now for the rest of the tour. Here's my bedroom." Just like its resident, the room was colorful and bright and fun. And messy.

"You were supposed to clean this up before you went for your sleepover," Molly said.

She sounded like every mother ever, Harry thought, his grin growing at how *normal* everything was. Just once, he would have loved for his father to comment on the state of his room. But William had never been around enough to notice anything like that.

Meanwhile, Aldwin was sniffing every shoe, every stuffed animal and pillow. Then he jumped up on Amelia's bed, walked in a circle, and settled himself down for a nap with his big head on his paws.

"Looks like he's found his spot already," Molly remarked.

"He thinks he's a fifteen-pound lapdog instead of a hundred-and-fifty-pound monster," Harry said. Knowing they were talking about him, Aldwin opened one eye. Amelia laughed. "When I first brought him home, I tried to keep him off the furniture, but it was no use."

"He must have been the cutest puppy," Molly said. "Cute but huge."

"I'm sure he was," Harry replied. "But I've only

had him a short while."

"Where was he before that?" Amelia looked terribly concerned as she put her arms around the dog's shoulders and rested her cheek on his fur.

"The folks at the animal shelter said he was well taken care of. Unfortunately, his previous owner was having health problems and couldn't manage his walks anymore. When her children couldn't take him in, she had no choice but to give him up. The shelter brought him to the farmer's market, and once I saw him, I had to take him home."

"He's very lucky you found him," Molly said in a soft voice. "Someone who doesn't care if he's a little over the hill. If his best years are behind him."

"Mom!" Amelia put her hands over Aldwin's ears. "He's still in the prime of his life."

But Harry had a feeling she hadn't been talking just about the dog. Though his twentysomething teaching assistant had been flirting with her, Harry guessed she didn't feel anywhere near as young as she looked. If he had raised a daughter by himself, he figured he'd feel much the same way.

Amelia gave Aldwin a kiss on his muzzle, then led Harry into a room just big enough for a double bed and a pine armoire. "This is going to be your room. We'll share the hall bathroom, but I call dibs on it between seven and seven thirty in the morning."

He held up his hands. "Don't worry. When we were kids, Suzanne taught me to stay out of her way until she was out the door in the morning."

"You could always use Mom's bathroom, if you needed to," Amelia offered.

Molly didn't say anything to that, but Harry couldn't imagine she would be too happy about his coming into her bedroom in only his boxers.

Unless she *would* be happy about it...

It wasn't easy to push the seductive thought away as they continued to the end of the hallway, but despite the fact that he felt more attracted to her than ever, figuring out how they were going to co-parent Amelia came first. Everything else—including finding out whether Molly's lips still tasted as sweet as they did in his memories—had to come second.

"This is Mom's bedroom and bathroom."

Molly's room wasn't large either, but it was a lovely and comfortable space, with French doors that looked out on the back garden. The sun was down now, but he could imagine light flooding in at sunrise.

It was nearly impossible to push away all the other things he could easily imagine, like being curled around Molly in the pine bed with the floral cover, their hastily stripped clothes on the floor, their hands, their mouths, their bodies insatiable for each other. Or in the bathtub together, with soap suds streaming over her naked skin while she straddled him, and he—

It was even harder to push the thoughts, the visions away this time.

"Why don't you show Harry the backyard and pick some veggies?" Molly suggested. "It's already pretty late, so we should get dinner on."

Understanding that Molly wasn't comfortable with his being in her bedroom—*Was that because she'd been envisioning the same sexy scenes?*—Harry followed Amelia into the backyard.

The garden was a remarkable space, even in twilight. Fruits and vegetables overflowed the wooden planter boxes, with ornamental flowers and shrubs surrounding the garden.

A sense of peace came over Harry. Not only because he was here with his daughter, but also because there was something so perfectly right about the garden, the cottage, the sounds of dogs barking and owls hooting.

All his life, he'd wondered what it would be like to have a "normal" family life. Of course he loved his siblings and his father, but boomeranging between the penthouse apartment on New York City's East Side and the house at Summer Lake, depending on who was having the bigger crisis, had never felt right.

Amelia hadn't had a father, but she had this peaceful cottage and yard and town. And, most important of all, she had a mother who loved her with everything she was.

As far as he was concerned, that made her the luckiest girl in the whole wide world.

"Do you know your way around a garden?" she asked.

"Nowhere near as well as you obviously do. Why don't you show me what's ripe and how to best harvest it?"

Harry had been a teacher for nearly his entire adult life. And when he'd thought about becoming a parent, he'd always assumed he'd be the one imparting knowledge to his child. But as his daughter taught him how to pluck the zucchini, he realized that *she* was going to be the one to teach *him* the most important things of all.

Not only how to be a good father, but also how to live with joy in every moment.

Even, he thought as he looked over his shoulder and saw Molly standing at the kitchen window, when life was utterly complicated.

But still stunningly beautiful.

CHAPTER ELEVEN

Tears pricked Molly's eyes as she watched Amelia and Harry in the garden. They were so good together, so comfortable with each other already.

As soon as he'd walked into her house, she'd been unable to see anything but him. He was big and broad, but that wasn't the reason he filled every one of her senses. His scent, the low rumble of his voice, the way he noticed everything around him—everything about Harry spoke to Molly, made her want, made her long for things she'd tried to make herself stop longing for years ago.

Now she was even less sure how this living arrangement was going to work. Not so much from a logistical standpoint—although there was the question of what exactly he was going to do all day while she was at work and Amelia was at school. No, it was more a question of how Molly was going to keep her emotions—and hormones—in check around him.

Because if she felt like a live wire after only twenty-four hours around Harry, then how was she going to deal with the steamy, shaky, desperate desire brewing inside of her after another full day had passed?

Both Amelia and Harry had an armful of produce as they walked into the kitchen, chatting and laughing. "Mom always cuts herself when she's on prep duty." Amelia put on an apron. "How are your knife-wielding skills, Dad?"

His eyes lit up, the way they did every time she called him *Dad*. "Though I'm better at swords, I actually know my way around a knife pretty well."

"He once won a throwing contest," Molly told her daughter, knowing she'd appreciate knowing a tidbit like that.

"No way."

"Way." But then Molly tried to adopt a serious expression. "You should never throw a knife."

"Duh." Amelia rolled her eyes. She turned back to Harry. "So how did you end up throwing them?"

"I used to participate in medieval-themed competitions."

"Again, your father is being way too modest," Molly said. "Harry didn't just *participate* in the competitions. He *won* them. Jousting, archery, colf—which is the ancestor of golf. Even horseshoes."

"Horseshoes?" Amelia giggled. "You've got a lot of layers, Dad."

Grinning at her compliment, he said, "Your mom

neglected to mention she was the queen of skittles."

"That's probably not a candy-eating contest, is it?"

"Nope." Molly laughed, glad to feel this relaxed with Harry in her kitchen when she'd been afraid she would feel anything but. "It's a really old ancestor of ten-pin bowling."

"That makes sense," Amelia said to Harry, "because Mom is a *killer* bowler. They're always trying to get her to join the league. I thought she should do it just to wear a retro bowling shirt with her name embroidered on it."

Harry turned to look at her. "You would look cute in one of those bowling outfits with *Molly* written on it."

Feeling herself flush, Molly said, "While you guys cook, I'm going to get out of your way." She wanted to look up how to add Harry's name to Amelia's birth certificate. Plus, Amelia and Harry surely needed as much one-on-one time together as possible to really cement their bond. "Holler when dinner's ready."

"Wait," Amelia said. "Before you go, we should take a selfie of our first dinner together." She gestured for Molly to come stand close to Harry, then squeezed in between them. "Say *cheese*."

"Cheese!"

After taking several shots, each of which seemed to require Harry and Molly to stand closer and closer together, Amelia looked at the phone and grinned. "Perfect." She showed Harry. "Don't you agree?"

Harry nodded, smiling at Molly as he said, "I sure do."

And the thing was, though Molly was still trying to get around all the massive changes in her and Amelia's lives, whenever Harry smiled at her, everything really *did* feel perfect.

The look in his eyes—as though he knew exactly what she was thinking—had her scurrying out of the kitchen. Hopefully, half an hour of Internet searching would settle her nerves, and her hormones, by the time they all sat down to dinner together.

* * *

No such luck.

It was just that having Sunday night dinner with both Amelia *and* Harry was so far outside the realm of any dreams Molly had ever had that she could barely eat a bite. How could she when she couldn't stop marveling over all that had come to be?

She hadn't eaten much since Harry's call the previous afternoon, but she could do little more than push her meal around her plate in exactly the way she'd taught Amelia not to.

Though Aldwin had a big bowl of dog food that Harry had brought from the city, Amelia kept sneaking bites of her meal to him under the table. When Harry did the same thing, Molly figured it must be okay. And marveled, yet again, at how they'd gotten here, to having what felt like a normal family dinner with the dog under the table.

Finally, when the plates were cleared and the dishes washed and put away, Molly decided it was the perfect time to show Harry something very important.

Her heart was thumping as she walked over to the tall bookshelf in the corner and pulled out a photo album. "This is the first photo album I put together when Amelia was born. There are more photos, obviously—" She gestured to the overstuffed shelf. "—but I thought this would be the best one to start with."

He took the photo album from Molly as though it was the most precious thing in the world. "Oh, Amelia," he said as he looked at the cover picture. She was three months old and grinning for all she was worth. "Look at you."

His words were thick with emotion, and Molly's heart clenched tight.

"You're absolutely beautiful. The most beautiful baby in the entire world."

"Really?" Amelia scrunched up her face as she looked at the picture, and even Aldwin leaned over to look. "Don't you think my head looks kind of huge? Like I'm an alien baby instead of human."

A laugh burst out of Molly, one she'd dearly needed. Amelia had a gift for making funny off-the-cuff comments. She hadn't won class clown in middle school for nothing. She also had a knack for knowing just what to do, just what to say, to lift people's spirits. Even a mother on the verge of breaking down in a torrent of tears over all the years, the memories, that Harry and Amelia had lost out on.

"I've told her a million times," Molly said to Harry in as normal a voice as she could manage, "that that's how big all babies' heads are."

He looked at the pictures more closely. "I guess it's a *little* on the huge side," he said, deadpan, "but if you ask me, it's still perfect. Although I should put on my glasses to make absolutely sure." He got up and took them out of his leather bag, which he'd brought inside earlier. "I usually only use these for reading, but I don't want to miss even the slightest detail of these photos."

Molly braced herself for impact, but once he turned back to them with the glasses on...

Oh. My. God.

She pretty much melted into the floor. She'd guessed he'd be the ultimate hot professor with the glasses, but it turned out that she'd far underestimated his geek-hotness factor.

Thank God he was so focused on the baby pictures that he didn't seem to notice the effect he was having on her.

He sat down again and picked up the photo album, opening it to a picture the nurse had taken of Molly a few minutes after she'd given birth, holding her newborn daughter swaddled in hospital blankets.

"Molly." His voice was hushed and raw with emotion as he looked up at her, then back at the picture.

She knew what he saw—how young she looked, how overwhelmed. But also, utterly radiant. And filled with determination to never, ever let her daughter down.

Molly's chest felt so tight she could barely breathe. "I should…" She ran out of air and had to try again. "I should let you two look at the album together."

"Wait, don't you want to tell Harry about the pictures?" Amelia protested.

"I would really appreciate it if you would," Harry agreed, pinning her with his dark, gorgeously bespectacled gaze. "Where did you have Amelia?"

"River Hospital here in Alexandria Bay. I was lucky to find the job at Boldt Castle during my pregnancy, and they had good health care at the local hospital."

"Tell him how many hours you were there trying to have me."

"Quite a few." Molly didn't think it would help to make a big deal out of every little thing he'd missed, even if being in labor for so long had been anything but little.

"Thirty-six hours!" Amelia liked making sure people had specific details for everything. Just like her father.

Harry looked horrified. "Was anyone there to help you?"

Molly went to get a glass of water from the sink so she didn't have to see his expression. "The nurses were great."

But though she couldn't see him, she could feel his frustration from where she stood. "I wish I could have been there for you."

Thankfully, before things got any more tense, Amelia pointed to another picture in the album. "I still have that stuffed pig. I'll go get it." She raced out of the room, with Aldwin so close on her heels he nearly tripped her. She came back a few moments later with a faded gray stuffed animal that only vaguely resembled a pig. "Mom says I sucked all the color out of it."

"That's the same stuffed animal?" Harry sounded incredulous.

Amelia nodded. "And I have footie pajamas that are almost identical to the ones I wore when I was a baby too."

"Speaking of pajamas," Molly said, knowing how tired her daughter must be when she herself was about to keel over at any moment, "you should probably get ready for bed, or getting up for school tomorrow is going to be rough."

After Amelia left the room, dog in tow, Molly was acutely aware of being alone with Harry. Sitting together on the couch looking at pictures together, it was almost as though they were a normal couple—one who had spent fifteen years together raising their daughter, rather than apart, never speaking, never getting to touch or kiss or hold each other.

Darn it, tears were coming again, just as Amelia came back into the living room looking adorable in her adult onesie pajamas, a teenager who thankfully didn't mind feeling like a little kid again sometimes.

"They look really comfortable. Do they sell those in my size?" Harry joked when she did a pirouette so that he could see just how well the outfit matched her baby clothes.

"Actually," Amelia said, "I think they do."

Molly could easily guess what Amelia was going to get Harry for Christmas. She also knew that he would somehow manage to look gorgeous and sexy in the pajamas, rather than as silly as any other man would have.

"Good night, Dad." Amelia leaned over to kiss Harry on the cheek and hug him.

Molly had never seen him look so close to tears—or so blissfully happy—all at the same time. "Good night, honey." He kissed and hugged her back.

Amelia was beaming as she came over to Molly, who pulled her into a tight embrace. "I love you, kid. You're amazing."

"So are you, Mom." Amelia was halfway out of the room when she turned back. "Oh, I wanted to ask— Dad, can you walk me to school tomorrow morning?"

"I wouldn't miss it."

"Great! We need to head out by seven thirty." She blew a kiss at them and was gone to join Aldwin in her bedroom.

"She hasn't let me drop her at school since she turned twelve," Molly remarked once Amelia had closed her door, trying to act as though he hadn't made her want to cry with his heartfelt reaction to the baby pictures in one moment...then jump him when she looked at him in his glasses the next. "She's obviously really looking forward to showing you off. Normally, she rides her bike or walks with a friend."

"I'm really looking forward to meeting her friends and teachers." As he spoke, he still looked a little emotionally overcome by Amelia's good-night kiss. "Do you know of anyone who could watch Aldwin for the day tomorrow?"

"A friend of mine owns a doggie day care a couple of blocks away," Molly said. "But why do you need someone to watch him?"

"Because I'd like you to come with us to her school tomorrow morning, and I'm not sure we should leave him alone in your house until we can be positive he won't go nuts pining for Amelia." He frowned as a thought occurred to him. "That is, if you can still get to work on time?"

She nodded. "You're right, I probably should go with you. If only to make sure Amelia actually gets to her first class on time, when I'm sure she won't want to let you go."

Just the way I never did.

* * *

After Molly sent a quick text to her friend about dropping Aldwin off in the morning, she said, "Before I head to bed, I wanted to chat with you about something."

Noting how serious she looked, he nodded. Strangely, she also looked relieved when he slid off his glasses. "Sure, what is it?"

"Now that we know for sure that you're Amelia's father, you should be on her birth certificate. I did a little research online while you were making dinner, and it looks like a fairly straightforward process. If you'd like, after we drop Amelia off at school, we could go to the Town Clerk's office to fill out the paperwork."

If Harry had any doubts about how badly Molly wanted to set things right, this erased them all. Not only did she want to make things official, she wanted it to happen as soon as possible.

"That would be great. But what about your job? You never know how long something is going to take in a government office. I'd hate for you to get in trouble with your boss."

"Stanley will understand, and there are a couple of people who can cover for me at the store on fairly short notice if we show up at the Clerk's office and there's a huge line. In any case, all of that takes second place to making sure you have legal custody rights. I don't want anyone to ever doubt that she's yours."

Despite the strange circumstances that had brought them here, it was really nice sitting in Molly's living room, talking as the stars twinkled outside the windows. Was this what they could have had all this time if they hadn't split up?

Fifteen years of nights on the couch together. Nights where he looked into her eyes and saw everything he wanted in their blue depths. Nights where he reached for her and pulled her close to feel her warm and soft and so damned sweet against him as they—

Molly suddenly jumped off the couch. Her skin was flushed, her lips rosy, as though he'd actually been kissing her instead of just fantasizing about it.

"It's late. I should go to bed. I'll check your room to make sure you have everything you need before I turn in."

But he couldn't let her go. Not yet. He reached for her hand and wrapped his around it. "This could have been so hard. But you're doing everything you can to make sure it isn't. Thank you, Molly. For doing such a great job with Amelia all these years, for letting me stay in your house, and for researching how to change the birth certificate."

And just for being you.

She gave him a tremulous smile, then pulled her hand from his and dashed out of the room.

Wanting nothing more than to go after her, Harry forced himself to pick up the photo album instead and take a seat in the armchair beside the bookshelf. Putting his glasses back on, he opened the album and lost his breath all over again at the beautiful photos of Amelia as an infant—and of Molly as a radiant young mother.

Every photo only made him more desperate to rewind time. To get a chance to do things over and get it right this time.

He traced his finger over a picture of Molly and Amelia by the water. Molly was wearing the baby on her chest in a wrap of some brightly colored fabric, and both of them had on hats that looked like they were about to fly off at any moment. Amelia's tiny hands were in Molly's.

Harry felt himself choke up as he wished that he could have been the one taking the picture all those years ago. But before any tears could fall, his gaze caught the photo on the facing page. Molly was holding Amelia up high, and the baby was laughing as her mother made a funny face at her.

Though he was still choked up, he couldn't stop smiling.

Molly had always been great at making faces. She'd never worried about not looking pretty. She'd just wanted to make the people she cared about happy.

Harry wasn't sure she'd ever realize just how happy she'd made him when they were eighteen. But even if she had, would that have made any difference when his family life had been such a mess?

He'd told Molly that sometimes the best thing to do was to look forward—and he'd meant it. But that didn't mean history wasn't important. Tonight, he was going to take this chance to go through these photo albums to learn about the history Amelia and Molly had built without him.

And then one day, if he was really lucky, maybe there would be a new photo album with him in it too.

* * *

Sleep came in fits and starts. Utterly exhausted, Molly had fallen asleep the moment her head had hit her pillow, but it hadn't lasted long. After she'd awakened a couple of hours later, she tossed and turned for so long she decided that getting up and making some hot tea and a snack might help her sleep.

Wrapping her robe around herself, she tiptoed out into the hall and was surprised to find Harry's bedroom door open—and his bed still made. She could hear dog and teenager snores coming from Amelia's bedroom across the hall.

But where was Harry?

She found him in the living room, fast asleep in the armchair, surrounded by photo albums. One was still open on his lap. His glasses, which he must have put back on after she went to bed, had fallen off and landed on it.

Walking quietly across the braided rug, she knelt beside him to see where he had stopped.

It was a photo taken when Amelia had won a prize from the county for the best poetry reading. Molly had her arms wrapped around her daughter, while Amelia proudly held up her trophy.

Molly remembered thinking how every sacrifice had been more than worth it, just to know that her daughter was so confident, so happy with who she was. Amelia would never let a boy—or anyone else—treat her badly, because she knew her own worth. It was the most important thing Molly could teach her.

Molly took the album off Harry's lap and put it back on the shelf. She was torn about whether to wake him. But she didn't want his neck and back to hurt the way hers would if she slept in a chair all night.

She put her hand on his arm and said, "Harry."

He had never been a very sound sleeper. Probably because he had always felt that he had to wake at a moment's notice if one of his family members needed him. But tonight she was having a heck of a time trying to wake him, going so far as putting her hands on his shoulders—his *very* broad shoulders—to give him a gentle shake.

His eyes finally opened, blurry with sleep. Likely, he would be wondering where he was. She was about to say something when he whispered, *"Molly."*

Her name was so full of longing, so full of desire, so full of passion, that she was held captive.

He lifted his hands to her face, cupping her cheeks, stroking her skin with the pads of his thumbs. "So beautiful," he murmured.

Then his lips were on hers, and he was kissing her.

And...oh God...why would anyone in their right mind want to stop a kiss like *this*?

His mouth was warm and sweet tasting from the fruit salad they'd had for dessert and, most of all, *desperate*.

He kissed her like he'd been waiting forever for the chance to kiss her again.

Like she was not only all he'd ever wanted, but all he would ever want again.

Like nothing but Molly mattered.

Like he never wanted to ever let her go.

Molly's head spun. With pleasure. With need. With a desperation that matched his.

It was impossible to keep from running her hands down from his shoulders to the strong muscles of his back, remembering with every inch she covered just how magnificent he'd been. And learning that he was even more so now.

Her gasps of pleasure were echoed by his groans, and when he moved to pull her onto his lap, there was nowhere else she could ever imagine wanting to be.

Until her foot struck the photo albums stacked beside the chair, and they fell one after the other onto the floor in a chorus of thumps that finally knocked a little sense back into her. Enough, at least, to make her realize that she needed to get off Harry's lap.

Especially given that he was staring at her as though he was wondering how she'd gotten there in the first place.

"Molly?" He said her name again, but this time it was a question. "You're real."

Oh no...

Had he been asleep the whole time?

For the best kiss of her life?

"You were asleep, and I was just trying to wake you up." Her words came out in a rush as she fumbled to get off him.

His hands tightened around her for a split second before he let her go. "I kissed you." He sounded a little shocked, which only made her flush hotter at what had just happened between them.

"I'm sure you didn't mean to," she said. "You must have been dreaming and—"

"You kissed me back."

She opened her mouth to respond, but nothing came out. What could she say? After all, it wasn't like *she* could claim dreaming as an excuse for her behavior.

In the end, all that came out was, "Don't worry, it won't happen again."

She hastily walked backward through the room, away from the greatest temptation she'd ever known, then lifted her hand in an awkward wave.

"Good night." She turned and fled back to her room with neither the tea nor the snack that she'd originally come out for, closing her door behind her, with a racing heart.

And lips that tingled from the best kiss of her life.

With the only man alive who could make her forget everything but him.

CHAPTER TWELVE

Monday morning, Molly woke to the smell of frying bacon. Mortification instantly flooded her cheeks at the memory of last night's kiss.

With only the slightest provocation, she'd thrown herself into Harry's arms. If the photo albums hadn't tipped over, who knew how things might have ended up? Would she have straddled him in the armchair and taken him the way she often had in college, barely stopping to throw their clothes aside before they were loving each other?

How would he act this morning? Would he want to talk about the kiss?

Or would he be okay with simply forgetting it?

Not that she would ever be able to forget, when just thinking about his kiss made her skin feel all tingly and overheated.

All her stomach cared about, however, was getting to the delicious-smelling food. Normally, school mornings were too hectic for more than splashing some cereal and milk in a bowl for breakfast before running out the door.

Was this what it was like to have a man in the house? Someone to pick up her slack, and then she could be there to pick up his?

She shouldn't let herself get used to this—not when she had no idea how long Harry would be staying. Especially if he was worried about her throwing herself at him every time he fell asleep. But her growling stomach still didn't want to listen to reason. Not when it smelled like a full fry-up was on offer—and she hadn't had one of those in forever. Even bone-deep embarrassment couldn't stand up to that kind of enticement.

She took the world's quickest shower, tried to blow-dry her hair and do her makeup at the same time, threw on a sky blue top, black skinny jeans, and ballet flats, then made herself walk at a normal pace into the kitchen when she wanted to run.

Just because of breakfast, of course.

Not because Harry was there. Not because even a handful of hours apart had felt like too long.

"Mom, can you believe Dad made all of this for us?" Amelia was already digging in. Aldwin lay at her feet, doing his usual silent prayer for bacon to fall into his mouth.

"It looks great," Molly said. She turned to Harry, trying not to flush a dozen shades of red after their never-should-have-happened kiss. "It's really nice of you to make us breakfast. But you didn't have to do that." Especially when she knew how late he'd stayed up looking at photos. All of which, she noted, had been neatly put away in the bookcase.

"I'm happy to pitch in any way I can." Though his words were light and easy, the intense, heated look in his eyes was anything but.

Warmth flooded her, and she ducked her head to hide her reaction from both Harry and her daughter.

"Thank you." Molly grabbed a plate and took a greedy amount of everything on offer. Not just bacon and eggs, but pancakes and toast too. She might not have been able to stomach much of anything the day before, but despite her mortification over last night's kiss, her hearty appetite had returned full force.

"I can't wait for my friends to meet you, Dad." Amelia was glowing with happiness. "I've gotten a million comments from everyone since posting that pic at the ice cream shop yesterday."

So had Molly. Her phone had been lighting up continuously since then with texts and emails and comments from friends and from people she barely knew, all of which she'd deliberately ignored. Once everyone met Harry live and in the drop-dead-gorgeous flesh, their curiosity was only going to grow.

She put down her fork, her appetite leaving again

as she thought about how difficult the next hour might be. This was her daughter's moment, and Molly didn't want to do anything to ruin it for her. She would just need to make sure she kept her discomfort over the situation from Amelia.

"I've got to grab my backpack, and then we should go," Amelia said, then headed into her bedroom with Aldwin at her heels.

Molly knew she and Harry were going to have to talk about the kiss in the light of day at some point, if only so that it didn't become the big elephant in the room whenever the three of them were together. But that would have to wait until Amelia was in class. First, she needed to prepare him for what to expect this morning.

"When we get to Amelia's school, it might be a little overwhelming." She took her plate over to the dishwasher. "After all," she added with what she hoped looked like a natural smile, "it's not every day someone's long-lost father shows up out of the blue."

"Whatever happens, I'm not worried about it." He brought over his own plate. "Are you?"

She shook her head. "No."

"Molly." He moved closer. "You don't have to say whatever you think the 'right thing' is. Not to me."

All it took was one look into his eyes and she couldn't hold back the truth. "Yes, I'm totally freaked out over it."

He brushed a lock of hair away from her cheek, making her breath catch. "Don't worry, I won't let anything bad happen. Not to Amelia or to you."

She swallowed hard, wishing she could believe him.

Wishing she could keep from falling for him all over again.

Wishing she could remember how much it had hurt the first time he didn't want her.

Wishing knowing how much *more* it would hurt the second time around would keep her from wanting to throw herself into his arms and kiss him senseless.

"Mom, Dad, are you ready?"

Molly jumped back, knocking her hip into the open dishwasher door. "I need to get my sweater from the bedroom."

What she really needed was to take a cold shower. Even though it wouldn't keep her cool for very long around Harry.

A few moments later, the three of them plus Aldwin were headed down the sidewalk, with Amelia giving Harry a verbal tour of town as they headed to the local doggy day care. "The boat launches and most of the restaurants are behind us. And that building—" Amelia pointed to their left. "—is the rec center where they have art classes."

Molly's friend Janet came out of the doggy day care to greet Aldwin, scratching him behind the ears. "Oh, don't you look like a sweetheart?"

"Janet, this is Harry. Harry, Janet will be taking care of Aldwin today while we're gone."

"Thanks so much." Harry shook her hand. "He's a pretty easygoing guy, although you're going to want to watch out for that tail once it gets wagging, especially if there are any puppies or small dogs around. He doesn't know his own strength."

Molly's heart melted a little bit more at how sweetly concerned Harry was about his dog.

"Don't worry about a thing." Janet motioned for Aldwin to sit, then once he had, gave him a treat. "He's going to fit right in with the rest of the gang."

They waved good-bye, then headed back down the street. Aldwin looked at Amelia's retreating back with sad eyes, but was soon distracted by a terrier that was being dropped off.

"My school is up ahead," Amelia said, continuing her tour, "and the town library is behind that. When I was little, we used to spend a lot of time there, especially when it was raining. It's still one of my favorite places to go."

"I've never been in a library I didn't like," Harry agreed.

"What's the library like in New York City?"

"Huge. But also small, if you know where to go. Next time we're there, I'll take you."

"Awesome." They rounded the corner to the front of the high school, where Amelia's friends and many of their parents were waiting. "You guys have to come meet my dad!"

A group of teenage girls descended on them, giggling and hair-flicking and wide-eyed.

"Dad, this is Jenny and Samantha and Lana and Clara."

As he shook everyone's hand, Molly could see that Amelia's friends were not only impressed with him, but a good number of them were practically swooning at his good looks as well. As were their mothers, who surrounded Molly while their girls chatted with Harry.

"What a huge surprise this is," Clara's mother, Janna, said. "I couldn't believe it when I saw Amelia's post on my phone and realized she'd finally found her dad. How are you doing? If it were me, I'd be completely freaking out."

Of course, I'm freaking out! I mean, look at him. I'm so far out of my depth here, you wouldn't believe it.

All Molly said, however, was, "I'm really happy that Amelia and Harry found each other."

"Oh yes," Janna agreed. "Harry looks like he's going to be an absolutely *wonderful* father."

The other women all nodded, with Jenny's mom,

Candice, saying to the others in a stage whisper, "I looked him up online and he's a brilliant academic. Single too."

Molly worked to fight back a horrible twinge of jealousy at the thought of Harry actually dating someone in town.

Lana's mother, Stacy, who looked like she'd put far more time than usual into her hair and makeup, asked, "How long will he be staying in town?"

Before Molly could reply, Samantha's voice carried over from Amelia's group of friends. "I'm confused. How come you didn't know Harry was your dad before now? Didn't your mom tell you?"

"She would have," Amelia replied, "but she had no idea there was even a chance that he could be my dad until I did one those DNA tests. We were all totally surprised."

Everyone turned to look at Molly, all of them clearly thinking the same thing—that the only way she could be surprised about Harry being Amelia's father was if she had been sleeping with more than one man at a time all those years ago.

In that moment, whatever good reputation she had built within the school community felt like it instantly crumbled. Though she wasn't about to justify her actions as an eighteen-year-old college student to anyone here, she still wanted to sink into a hole in the ground and let it swallow her up.

As though he could see straight inside her heart, Harry came to put his arm around Amelia's—and Molly's—waists. "I couldn't be happier to find out that Amelia is my daughter…and also to be back in Molly's life after all this time."

"It really is the greatest thing that's ever happened!" Amelia agreed.

Molly admired how matter-of-fact Amelia was, how resilient and positive. Instead of focusing on what she'd missed, she was solely focused on everything she'd *gained*. Namely, a new dad who clearly wanted to be there for her in any and every way that he could.

Molly wanted so badly to follow her daughter's example—and Harry's too—and look only on the bright side. Allow herself to start fresh. But she didn't know how to forget the past.

Or whether she even should.

Not that she would be able to gloss over their past any time soon, when she had a feeling everyone in town was going to keep asking her about it until they all knew the full story.

Harry's arm tightened around her waist, and when he smiled at her, for a moment everything seemed so much better.

"If there's time before the first bell rings, Amelia, I'd love to meet your teachers."

Molly barely held back her sigh of relief. They would see the other parents again at *The Sound of Music* that weekend, but between now and then she hoped some of the hysteria over her family situation would have died down.

She thought Harry would let go of her when Amelia led them toward her English class, but he kept his arm around her, leaning close to whisper in her ear, "You're doing great."

Though she appreciated his support, they both knew that she was barely hanging on. Here she thought she'd be the one to smooth over Harry's introduction to people in town, only to have Harry be the one taking care of her. Just the way he had always taken care of everyone around him.

Soon, Harry was surrounded again, this time by Amelia's teachers, most of whom did a far better job of hiding their surprise at his out-of-the-blue appearance than the mothers had.

Molly supposed teachers saw pretty much everything at one point or another. Then again, one of their students finding her father via an online DNA test—which Amelia was explaining to her science teacher at that very moment—might very well take the cake.

* * *

"I'm really sorry about that," Molly said as they left the

high school campus and headed on foot to the Town Clerk's office. "For a moment there, I thought some of the moms were going to start stuffing their telephone numbers into your pockets. Everyone is actually really nice. They must all be so surprised by our news."

"They were just being friendly."

She laughed, one of his favorite sounds in the world. "Sounds like you have a different definition of *friendly* than I do. In any case, now that we've dealt with the schoolyard, I'll just have to deal with everyone at work asking a million questions about you."

"Why don't I meet them in person today? That way, I can also see where you work."

"Today?" She licked her lips. "Don't you have things to take care of for your own job?"

"I checked email before breakfast, and Kelsin said he had everything under control for my classes. And until you or Amelia look at my book and give me feedback, the last thing I want to do is open the file and stare at a blinking cursor for hours. Which means I'm free to head over to Boldt Castle with you after we're done filing our paperwork for the new birth certificate. You can even put me to work so that I'm not hanging around, being in your way."

"It's inventory day. I usually like my job, but inventory is literally the most boring thing a human being can do. For eight hours straight." Each sentence was another gauntlet laid down, all clearly intended to put him off coming with her. "You're going to hate it."

"Maybe." He shrugged. "But I'd still like to see where you work and help out if I can."

"I'd forgotten how stubborn you can be."

He grinned. "Anything else you need me to remind you about?"

She shook her head and stepped away from him so fast that she nearly stumbled. "No." She picked up the pace. "We'd better get a move on or the line at the Clerk's office is going to get really long."

As she practically speed-walked beside him, he silently noted that she hadn't brought up last night's kiss. He truly had been half asleep when it happened. Just far enough outside of reality to believe he was still dreaming…and to let himself reach for her the way he'd wanted to since the moment he'd set eyes on her again.

She'd been even sweeter than he remembered— and had seemed as hungry as he was to touch and be touched, to press close and relish their undeniable heat and hunger.

Unfortunately, given the way she'd jumped out of his arms, she was probably hoping he'd forget it ever happened.

Not a chance.

Harry knew people thought he'd been blessed with

above-average intelligence. But they were wrong. What he had in spades was the ability to focus, to concentrate on something until he had it figured out from every angle.

Right now, he wasn't at all concerned with the classes he'd passed off to his teaching assistant, or the book he was supposed to be writing. Instead, every ounce of his focus was on forming a strong bond with his daughter.

And finding out if the kiss he and Molly had shared might be the perfect beginning of a second chance at love.

CHAPTER THIRTEEN

Harry had figured they'd be stuck in Alexandria Bay's administrative building for most of the morning. Fortunately, taking care of official paperwork in a small town was radically different—and far more expeditious—than it was in New York City. In less than thirty minutes, they had filled out the Acknowledgment of Paternity form, submitted a copy of the original birth certificate along with the two DNA test results, and paid their fee, with the assurance that as long as everything checked out, the new birth certificate would soon be in the mail.

They caught the next ferry to Boldt Castle, and yet again, Harry was bowled over by the beauty of the area. Not only from the large trees that surrounded the waterfront homes, and the impressive-looking castle toward which they were speeding, but also the quality of light reflecting off the water.

But Molly's beauty outshone it all.

Once upon a time, he would have told her that. But given how determined she seemed about keeping their relationship platonic, and despite the undeniable heat between them, he was afraid she would think it was only a cheesy pickup line.

The next time they kissed, there wouldn't be any confusion. There had already been far too much of that.

"I always thought my office was in a good location, but this—" He turned to take it all in, the lush foliage, the bright blue water, the boats, and the backdrop of the castle. "This is spectacular."

"It really is." They disembarked, and Molly led him down the walkway toward the gift shop. "You'd think that after fifteen years the shine might have worn off, but it hasn't. I still have to pinch myself to believe I really work here. The only downside is that in an emergency it's harder to get to Amelia, although my boss has always been really flexible with my schedule. I can set up my hours around whichever after-school program or sports team she's on. And I've been lucky that so many people are happy to help on the mainland." She half laughed as she added, "You actually met some of them this morning. Like I said, they really are a great bunch. Just a little star struck by you."

"No one's ever been star struck by me before. This must be how Smith and Ryan and Drake feel," he joked. His cousin Smith was a movie star. Ryan was a pro baseball player. And his brother Drake was a well-known painter. Harry didn't mention his father, however, who was quite possibly the most famous of them all.

"Are you kidding?" Molly asked. "Even when we were in college, people were constantly stumbling over themselves to impress you and get you to notice them."

"That has nothing to do with me. That's because of my father and my family history."

"No," she insisted. "You've always been brilliant and charismatic. It's because of who *you* are, Harry, not because of who you're related to."

"That's nice of you to say, even if I'm still not sure I'll ever see it that way. Honestly, it's not always easy to figure out where my family ends and I begin." The sentiment was one he'd never revealed to anyone before.

"Once I had Amelia," Molly said, "I finally understood how it feels to be so connected to another person. I mean, you and I were really close for a while in college. But I always knew that you would be okay without me because you had your whole huge family all over the world. Whereas with Amelia, she needed me in a way no one else ever had before. And I needed her just as much. Which is why, if I'm being totally honest, the idea of her growing up and making a life for herself, by herself, kind of freaks me out. Taking the

DNA test, going off on the bus to see you—all that is part of her becoming her own person."

"I know exactly what you mean. My brothers and sister needed me for so long that now that they're all happily settled, sometimes I find myself at loose ends." He held her gaze. "Seeing them all so in love makes me wonder about my own happily-ever-after."

Her eyes widened, but she didn't look away. "There's no one in the city who…" She looked as though she was trying to find the right way to put it. Finally, she settled on, "Who makes you happy?"

"No." He was very glad she wanted to know if he was free. "No one."

"I'm sure—" Her breath seemed to catch in her throat. "I'm sure you'll find someone soon."

He wanted to move closer, wanted to take her hand in his, wanted to say, *I already have—it's you.* "What about you? Is there anyone special in town who's going to beat me up for staying with you?"

"No."

Though it was nearly impossible, he didn't allow himself to touch her, or kiss her. He only said, "Good."

When she jumped away as though he *had* kissed her, he knew they not only needed to talk about what had happened when she'd woken him up in the living room—he also needed her to know what it had meant to him.

"Last night when we kissed, I might have thought I was dreaming at first. But that's only because I have wanted to kiss you nearly every moment since I set eyes on you again."

"Harry…" He thought he could read longing, and desire, in her eyes. Too soon, though, they were shrouded by doubt. "I thought we both agreed that last night was a mistake. And it shouldn't happen again."

"Just because I didn't stop you from running away doesn't mean I agreed."

Her shoulders went back, her chin up. "I didn't run."

He couldn't keep his mouth from quirking up slightly at the corner. She was even more beautiful when she was facing off against him.

"Okay, maybe you didn't actually break into a run. But you were definitely intent on getting away from me—and making sure there'd be no more kisses." Back in college, he wouldn't have pushed her on any of this. But back then, he hadn't known just how much it would hurt to lose her. Now that he did, he wouldn't hold back on the difficult questions. "Why?"

"Amelia's happiness is the only thing that matters. And whatever we do…" Molly paused, licking her lips, which only brought more of Harry's attention to them and how badly he wanted to kiss her again. "I don't want either of us to do anything to change that."

"I agree that nothing is more important than Amelia." But before he could say that he wasn't at all sure that also meant keeping his distance from Molly, given the fact that Amelia seemed perfectly happy to throw the two of them together, a tall woman with white-blond hair and a flowing dress flung open a back door that looked like it led into the gift shop.

"There you are, Molly! And you have someone with you." The woman gave him a serious once-over that told him she was most definitely taking his measure.

"Sorry I'm late," Molly said. "Did you and Stanley get my text this morning letting you know I'd be a little late?"

"We did, and you're here sooner than I thought." Turning to Harry, she held out a hand. "I'm Greta. And Molly has told me absolutely *nothing* about you. Although I did see a picture Amelia posted with a rather surprising hashtag attached to it."

He grinned, liking her immensely. She reminded him of his Aunt Mary—lovely and strong, with a ready smile and a quick handshake. "I'm Harry Sullivan. Amelia's father."

As Molly filled Greta in, Harry could see that they were very close. Where Molly had seemed slightly embarrassed by the revelations in front of everyone at Amelia's school, she was matter-of-fact with Greta.

"I wanted to call you and Stanley to let you know in person, rather than having you find out over social media," Molly said, "but there hasn't been time."

"I'll say there hasn't!" The next thing Harry knew, Greta was hugging him. As soon as she let him go, she said, "I know how much Stanley wants to meet you. As soon as his morning donor meeting is finished, he'll come by." She waved over the other staff members. "Everyone, Molly has someone she would like all of you to meet."

"She's a force of nature," Molly said with a fond shake of her head as Greta rounded everyone up.

"One who obviously cares very much for you and Amelia."

"Over the years, Greta and Stanley became the parents—and the grandparents—that my real parents never seemed to want to be." Amelia had told him in the car on their drive from the city that she'd seen her grandparents only a handful of times over the years, and only for a few hours at each visit. "I owe them more than I can ever repay."

"Everything Greta and her husband have done for you, they've done because they love you both."

Over the next several minutes, Harry met people from all wings of the castle—the store, the ticket booth, the ferry staff, the groundskeepers. All of whom clearly adored Molly.

She might not have grown up with a big family, but she'd found one here.

Finally, everyone went back to their posts, the doors opened, and the first visitors of the day walked in, looking for coffee and souvenirs.

"Are you sure you don't want to take the ferry back?" Molly asked him. "You should be writing your soon-to-be Pulitzer Prize winning book, not helping me with inventory."

Didn't she know? He would do anything to be near her.

Perhaps he should have been surprised that it hadn't taken him long to get to that place. But he'd fallen in love with Molly once, so falling for her all over again now that she was even stronger, wiser, and more beautiful than she'd been at eighteen, made perfect sense to him. What's more, she was a hell of a mother. To Harry, that counted for pretty much everything.

"At this point," he replied, "all I've got are thirty thousand words strung together that don't say much of anything. Believe me, I'd *much* rather help you with inventory."

"If you meant it about having Amelia look at your draft, I know she'll be thrilled."

"Of course I meant it. And I want you too, Molly."

Her eyes grew big, her pupils dilating. Just the way they had after their kiss last night.

He could have clarified his statement by making it clear that he was talking about her help with the book. Deliberately, he didn't.

Because he wasn't.

The only way they were going to find out if they could make things work a second time was if they didn't fight it every step of the way. Last night's kiss had already proven that their attraction had gotten only hotter since they'd last been together. Hopefully, constant little reminders of how good they were together would provide even more proof.

"Tell me," he said, once she'd handed him a tablet with a digital spreadsheet and instructions to begin counting Boldt Castle snow globes, "how did you pick Alexandria Bay when you left New York City?" Thinking about the asshole who had threatened to make her get rid of her baby—*Harry's* baby—made his hand clench on the side of the tablet.

"I don't know if you remember, but the book you helped me take down the first day we met was about Boldt Castle."

"All I remember is you. Standing in the middle of the stacks. You were the most beautiful woman I'd ever seen." Again, he didn't hold back as he added, "You still are."

Though she tried to hide the flushing of her skin with the fall of her hair, he still noticed.

"Anyway," she continued as though he hadn't just sent her heart racing, which he very much hoped he had, "the story of how Boldt Castle came to be always spoke to me. So when I had to find somewhere to go, I figured this was a good place to start looking. I took the same bus ride that Amelia did on Saturday, albeit in the opposite direction. Greta is the one who interviewed me that first day. I started work the next morning and never left."

Because Harry was a history professor, people often thought that meant he knew everything about, well, everything. Which was far from true. Even, he was slightly embarrassed to admit, when it came to his own state.

"Tell me the story of Boldt Castle."

Her eyes lit up, the way they always had in college when they were discussing history. "George C. Boldt was the owner of the Waldorf Astoria hotel. He wanted to build a castle here on Heart Island, not to show off how wealthy he was, but as a grand display of love for his wife, Louise."

No wonder Molly had been so intrigued by the castle. While Harry had always focused on logistics and maps and plans, she had been far more interested in the famous love stories through time. What's more, telling him this story was the first time she'd completely relaxed around him. Harry hoped it was the beginning of her letting down her guard for good.

"Construction began in 1900," she continued. "Three hundred workers built the six-story, 120-room castle. As I'm sure you must already know based on your knowledge of the medieval period, it was patterned after buildings of the sixteenth century, when classical details were applied to the towered, medieval forms. Integral to the design are its tunnels, the powerhouse, the Italian gardens, a drawbridge, a tower, and a dovecote."

"It's very impressive. But wasn't it shut down for several decades?"

"Longer than that. In January of 1904, Boldt sent a telegram to the island, instructing the workers to stop construction immediately." Her face fell, even though she was recounting someone else's tragedy, rather than her own. "His wife had died suddenly, and he was utterly brokenhearted. He never returned to the island."

"My father didn't build my mother a castle," Harry found himself saying, "but he would have if he could. She was his everything. And when she died..." He shook his head. "Well, this is the part everyone knows—he never painted again." Harry rarely spoke about his parents' history to anyone. He figured they could get all they needed from the Internet. Even with Molly, he'd rarely divulged much of their history. But the parallels were too strong for him to keep quiet. "This castle was essentially Boldt's final painting for his wife, wasn't it?"

"It was." Molly's voice was soft and full of empathy. "I'm sorry, Harry, for what you and your siblings and your father went through."

His gut twisted, and he worked to push the emotion down, the way he always had. "It all happened a long time ago."

"So did this. But it's still important."

When she looked as though she wanted to say more, he asked, "What happened next? How did the castle become a historic site?"

His attempt to divert her attention back to the castle, away from his family, had no finesse. Thankfully, however, she didn't press him further on his parents, but simply answered his question.

"For seventy-three years, the castle and the other structures stood at the mercy of the wind, rain, ice, and snow. And especially vandals. This was a heck of a place to bring a date for a little one-on-one time back in the day, if you know what I mean."

He laughed, the tightness in his chest from talking about his parents loosening. "Let me guess the favorite place to go." He pointed out the window. "The tower."

"Wow, you're good."

He grinned. "I was just thinking about where I would have taken you."

Again, she flushed, her skin going beautifully rosy. Only the fact that they were still in the gift shop, her co-workers surrounding them, kept him from kissing her this time.

"As I was saying, in 1977 the Thousand Island Bridge Authority acquired the property and has been rehabilitating and restoring the Heart Island structures ever since."

"It really is a hell of a story. I know we're chained to our inventory tablets today, but I'm hoping you'll be able to give me a tour sometime soon."

"Of course I will. You're especially going to love the historical archives. We've done a lot to organize and fill them out over the past few years."

Amelia had told him that Molly did volunteer work in the archives. Why wasn't she running them? Just because she hadn't yet finished her undergraduate degree didn't mean she wasn't already hugely qualified for the position. The way she'd told him the origin story had captivated him.

"Have you ever thought of writing a book about the castle?"

She looked at him as if he were crazy. "Who would want to read a book about Boldt Castle written by a non-historian?"

"I would."

"I'm sure prospective publishers would be impressed to know I've got one guaranteed sale," she said in a self-deprecating tone.

He couldn't help but notice, however, what she *hadn't* said.

"You have an idea, don't you?"

"After fifteen years of working here, who wouldn't have ideas?"

"Plenty of people. What is it?"

"Tell me about your family," she said instead. "It's been so long since I've last seen them, and it sounds like they're all doing so well."

"I'll be happy to tell you. After you answer my question."

"Everyone thinks you're so mild-mannered," she muttered. "If only they knew the truth."

He grinned, knowing he had her. At least, on this front. "I'll be here for a full day of inventory, so…"

She made a sound of frustration, one so adorable he nearly laughed out loud.

"Okay, okay. You can stop with the full-court press. I *do* have an idea, but it isn't straight history. It's historical fiction. Based on the facts and the real-life people, but more of an in-depth look into their emotions and lives, rather than the nuts and bolts of getting this place built and then later restoring it. There's just so much richly layered history to jump from, especially the beautiful love letters we have in the archives."

"You need to write your book, Molly."

"Thank you for the vote of encouragement. Now, tell me about your family. There was an exhibition of Drake's paintings here a few years ago. I could hardly believe the scrawny high school kid I knew had created something so amazing."

Harry was extremely proud of his siblings, but he wanted to talk more about her book idea, wanted to suggest that they could help each other. She could read through his draft and notes, and he could do the same for her.

All of which assumed he'd be staying in Alexandria Bay.

He'd always loved New York City. But living here, surrounded by so much water, didn't sound bad at all. Especially if it meant he could be close to both Amelia and Molly.

But he knew better than to push her too hard, too fast. Not yet, anyway.

Finally answering her question, Harry said with a laugh, "Drake definitely isn't scrawny anymore. Of the four of us, he's the biggest. And so damned talented, I can hardly believe I'm related to him sometimes."

"You said he recently got engaged. What is his fiancée like?"

Clearly, she didn't follow the online gossip sites. Then again, when would she have the time, between work, raising her daughter, and getting her degree? "Rosa was on a reality TV show for several years. She got caught in a bad spot with some pictures that were illegally taken and leaked to the press."

Molly frowned. "I remember Amelia and her friends talking about that. I felt really bad for her—and I couldn't help but think how furious I would be if she were my daughter. I didn't realize she was dating Drake, though."

"She wasn't, at least not when it happened. She met Drake right after the pictures went public. He helped her in any way he could. And she helped him too, with his painter's block."

"That couldn't have been fun for him."

"I don't imagine it was, although he wasn't exactly forthcoming about it to any of us."

"It can be hard to ask for help. Even from the people closest to you."

Her words echoed his sister's closely enough that it gave Harry pause. "Suzanne is just as brilliant as we all knew she was. She founded a digital security company. You probably use her products—they're the industry standard for computers and phones."

"You must be so proud, Harry. Especially after all you did to make sure nothing fell through the cracks for your sister and brother in high school."

Very few people knew what Harry's life had been like back then. That he'd been mother and father, tutor and coach.

"They're worth it."

"Of course they are." She looked up from the shelf of wooden boats she was counting. "You said Suzanne is also engaged?"

He nodded. "Roman was her security guard—the guy Drake, Alec, and I had to hire when her company was facing some major threats that she didn't seem to be taking seriously enough."

"Is she all right?"

"She's great, thankfully."

"Thank God. I'm guessing she was none too thrilled when you hired a bodyguard to protect her...and that you and your brothers were even *less* thrilled when their relationship turned into romance."

"Right on all counts. Especially for Alec." Harry grimaced. "To be honest, he's still getting his head around their relationship."

"What about you?"

"Roman is a great guy. No one will ever be good enough for my sister, but he comes pretty darn close."

"If you're that protective about your sister, you're totally going to freak out about your daughter."

Panic seized him. As a new father, there was so

much to think about. Honestly, this felt like one of the most daunting of them all. "Amelia isn't already dating, is she?"

"Not yet. But she probably will soon. And I'm—" She stopped to correct herself. "*We* are going to have to figure out a way to deal with it."

"We could forbid her to date until college."

"Forbidding her to do anything is a one-way ticket to trouble. You obviously have a lot to learn about teenagers." Molly immediately looked stricken. "Sorry, I didn't mean for it to come out like that. Not when I know how badly you would have wanted to be with her all these years."

He put his hand over hers, where she was holding a stuffed river otter. "Like I said last night, we can't go back and change the past. What happened happened. And sometimes you, or I, or Amelia, or a friend or family member, or even a stranger, is going to say something that makes it hurt all over again. Maybe even a lot of times."

"I just don't know how to stop wishing things could have been different."

"I've been wishing for that my entire life," he found himself saying.

A silence fell between them. Not an uncomfortable one, exactly. More pensive, on both their parts.

"Now on to Alec," he finally said. "His story is one

you're going to find hard to believe. Although after everything you, Amelia, and I have just been through, maybe you won't."

"Did he unknowingly father a daughter too?" Molly looked like she was holding her breath waiting for his answer.

"No. At least I don't think so. But his business partner had a daughter, one he gave up for adoption right after she was born. No one knew about Cordelia, not even Alec. Unfortunately, when Gordon had a heart attack and the paramedics were unable to save him, Alec learned that Cordelia had inherited half of the company from the birth father she'd never met."

"Before the past couple of days, I probably would have said your story sounds like something you couldn't make up if you tried. Now I'm starting to wonder if things like this happen more than I ever thought they did."

"Probably," he agreed. "Fortunately, Alec and Cordelia's story has a happy ending. So happy, in fact, that now they're married."

"Alec is married?" Molly shook her head. "You already said that he's given up big business to be a chef, which is surprising enough. But of everything you told me, hearing that he's married really is the most difficult one to wrap my head around. He was always such a ladies' man. And so…"

She obviously didn't want to finish her sentence, so Harry did it for her. "Troubled?"

"Well, yes. He seemed to have so many demons."

"He did. Most of them revolving around my mother and father." Every conversation they had today seemed to lead right back to them. "Amazingly, Alec and Dad have finally patched things up."

"That's fantastic." But Molly suddenly looked a little nervous. Harry understood why as soon as she said, "What about you and your father? How are things between you two now?" She hastily added, "Better, I hope."

"They were always fine." It was a knee-jerk reaction for Harry to act as though everything had always been okay. But it was pointless when Molly, of all people, knew better. "What I mean is that my father and I never had any ill will toward each other."

"I know you didn't." He got the feeling she was picking each word with extreme care. "Although he did used to depend quite heavily on you." She paused, shaking her head. "Never mind, it's none of my business."

But now that William was Amelia's grandfather, regardless of whether anything ever happened between Harry and Molly again, it *was* her business. "Things remained pretty rough for Dad for quite a while. Right up until Drake met Rosa, actually. Drake needed to take her somewhere she could escape from the press for a while, so he took her to the house at Summer Lake. I don't know if it was watching Drake fall in love for the first time, or if Rosa reminded Dad of my mother in some way...but Dad really pulled it together for them. Then again with Suzanne and Roman. And when he had a heart attack—" Molly gasped, and he quickly said, "Don't worry, he's doing great."

"Thank God."

"In the hospital while Dad was recovering, he and Alec were finally able to talk. Really talk for once. And, I think, to forgive."

"That's huge."

"It is," Harry agreed. "Like I said before, everyone in my family seems settled. Happy. Content." He had to laugh. "I should have guessed it would be my turn for a little drama."

"Trust me, having a teenage daughter means you're in for *way* more than a *little* drama. Sometimes life with Amelia feels like twenty-four-seven drama. But despite the headaches, I wouldn't have it any other way."

"I know I've only been in Amelia's life for two days, but I already feel that. As though I wouldn't change one single thing, wouldn't wish for even the truly painful moments to be erased, if having to make my way through them means I get to be her father now."

"I truly am happy that Amelia found you." She looked into his eyes, her heart in hers. "I'm so glad you're part of our family now, Harry."

Nothing could have stopped him from pulling Molly into his arms. Not the way she kept trying to fight their attraction, not the mistakes they'd both made in the past, not the other people in the room who might be watching. He simply needed to feel her heart beat against his.

And when she hugged him back just as tightly, he hoped it was because she needed the same thing.

CHAPTER FOURTEEN

"Molly, I hear there's someone you want to introduce me to!"

Stanley's voice boomed through the gift shop. But this time, instead of jumping away from Harry, Molly could barely make herself shift out of the circle of his arms. Every time he touched her, another part of her heart lit up that she'd thought would remain forever dark.

She felt his hand stroke her hair, and then they separated. Only, as soon as they were apart, she wanted to reach for his hand again.

Just because she knew better than to start another romantic relationship with Harry, that didn't mean they couldn't be friends, did it? In fact, wouldn't it be best for Amelia if they were?

Pushing away the thought that being *just friends* with Harry was bound to be impossible, when it wasn't only her heart lighting up whenever he touched her, she turned to Stanley. "I'd like to introduce you to Harry Sullivan, Amelia's father. Harry, this is Stanley, my boss and my good friend."

The two men shook hands, then Stanley said, "Greta filled me in on some of the details. Sounds like both of you have been thrown on a roller coaster right at the loop-de-loop."

"That's *exactly* what it feels like," Molly agreed.

"You could have called us, you know. We would have dropped everything to be there for you."

"You and Greta are both so sweet to offer." She'd spent so long going it alone, that even after years as part of a generous community, it was still hard to remember she could ask people for help—and that they would come. "You won't be surprised to hear that Amelia is absolutely thrilled."

"I'm sure she is, finding out her father isn't some deadbeat, after all." Stanley turned back to Harry. "Unless you're a deadbeat who scrubs up real good, that is. What do you do for a living?"

"I teach history at Columbia. At least, I did until yesterday, when I took a leave of absence."

"To come here and be with Amelia and Molly?"

"Yes, sir."

"Any other children? Wife or girlfriend?"

"No, sir, on both counts."

Molly had never been in a situation like this, where her father vetted a potential suitor.

Okay, so Stanley wasn't actually her father—and

she and Harry weren't dating. But from where she was standing, it still felt the same. Embarrassing…and also really nice. Just to have someone care about her enough to look after her.

At last, Stanley softened toward Harry. "You be sure to let Greta and me know if you need anything. We've always looked out for Molly and Amelia—at least, when they'll let us. We'll do the same for you."

"Thank you." Harry looked at her and smiled. "Fortunately, the three of us seem to be doing a good job so far of working things out as they come up."

"In that case," Stanley said, "maybe you can help convince Molly to take my offer."

"Which offer is that?"

"Stanley—"

He plowed on despite Molly's attempt to stop him. "Our historical archivist has recently left to work in Europe. I've been after Molly to take the job, but she keeps turning me down."

"Stanley," Molly said again, "we've already talked about this. You don't need to bring Harry into it."

"I wouldn't need to bring him into it, if you would just see sense!" Stanley's voice boomed out, loudly enough that several customers looked over to see what the commotion was about. "You're great at managing the store, and you've been instrumental in helping us keep on top of the latest digital technologies. But we both know where your heart really lies. With history, not retail. And no one is more enthusiastic about the history of Boldt Castle than you are."

Greta called from across the room, "Stanley, your next meeting started five minutes ago."

"Darn it, the donors are going to get restless if I'm gone any longer. But I'm not letting you off the hook with this, Molly." He put a hand on Harry's shoulder. "I hope you won't either."

As soon as Stanley walked away, Molly picked up her tablet and started counting coloring books. But when she kept losing count, she knew it was no use trying to concentrate. Not with Harry's gaze trained on her. And not when she knew exactly what he wanted to say.

Before he could ask why she hadn't taken the job, she said, "It's more hours, and I'd need to travel to conferences throughout the year, which won't work because I need to be here for Amelia."

"Does she know they've offered you the job?"

"No. I asked Stanley and Greta not to mention it. I don't want her to think she's holding me back. I guarantee she'd be all over me to take the job if she knew about it."

"Of course she would. Because she loves you, she wants you to be happy, and she knows it's exactly the right fit for you."

"I've already told you why I can't do it! Who is going to be there for Amelia if I'm not?"

"I am," he said simply. "I know you've had to be both mother and father to her for fifteen years, but I'm here now."

"For how long?"

For a moment, she held her breath, hoping he might say *forever*. But she knew better than that, knew that even if he did, it wouldn't necessarily mean anything. Just because people wanted to make promises like that, didn't mean it was always possible to keep them.

"I won't leave Amelia. Not now that I've found her." He moved closer and lowered his voice. "And I don't want to leave you again, Molly. I never wanted to leave you in college either. I'm so sorry that I did."

Her chest felt so tight she could hardly breathe. "We've already talked about this. You did what you had to do."

"And this time, I'm going to do what I *want* to do."

She was caught in his eyes, in his words, already wrapped up in his spell. Right smack dab in the romantic dreams she'd once had. Dreams she knew better than to believe in.

She decided it would be best to approach this from a wholly sensible standpoint. "What about your job? You worked hard to get where you are."

"I'm not worried about my job. I have tenure, which means I can take some time to research and write. And if I want to get back into the classroom, I'm sure I can teach at a sister university nearby."

Since *sensible* hadn't worked, she had to remind him, and herself, "We have to think about Amelia. You can't do anything—*we* can't do anything that could hurt her."

"Do you really think my falling back in love with her mother will hurt her?"

Molly opened her mouth to reply, but nothing came out. How could it, when she had no idea how to respond? No idea what to think, or how to feel, after hearing Harry say that he might be falling in love with her again.

"How's inventory going over there?" Greta called from behind the register.

Her friend must have noticed her fumbling from across the room and was trying to save her. But whether from Harry, or from herself, Molly honestly didn't know.

"I'm guessing that's my cue to get back to work and give you a breather." But before he walked away, he leaned in close and said, "I meant every word, Molly. I'm not here for a vacation. And I'm not here to play at being a father. Now that I've found my daughter—and now that I've found you again—I'm here to stay."

★ ★ ★

Epiphanies, Harry now realized, were funny things. They didn't creep up on you, so much as bash you over the head with an emotional two-by-four.

Manhattan had been his home for more than three decades. Less than twenty-four hours ago, he'd packed a bag so that he could be with his daughter in Alexandria Bay.

Harry had never been the crazy Sullivan. He'd never been the impetuous one. And he'd certainly never been the one who wore his heart on his sleeve. Yet, already he knew that this was where he would be staying for good. He wouldn't regret giving up his job, if it came to that. He wouldn't regret leaving behind a successful career. He wouldn't regret leaving the nonstop activity of the city for the slow, quiet pace of a small town.

The only thing he would regret was not being there one hundred percent for Amelia.

And not giving every last piece of his heart to Molly.

He'd made so many mistakes when it came to love. In college, he hadn't had enough faith in his relationship with Molly, hadn't believed they could stay the course.

But Amelia had changed everything. Not only by ringing his doorbell and giving him the best news of his life, but by proving to him that Molly had the most steady, most faithful heart of anyone he'd ever known.

Molly was his first love.

Harry knew without a shadow of a doubt that she would be his last.

CHAPTER FIFTEEN

Harry didn't get a chance to speak with Molly again until they were heading home on the ferry that afternoon. While he had continued doing inventory, she had been pulled in half a dozen directions, with someone from nearly every department coming at some point throughout the day to ask her for help with a wide variety of issues.

Stanley hadn't been exaggerating when he'd said Molly was the expert on Boldt Castle. From the donors with whom she'd been asked to have lunch, to helping the onsite handyman, she could pinpoint the exact day in history when the tower construction had begun *and* knew exactly where to look for a rare hinge needed to re-hang an antique door.

Since he'd been left to his own devices, Greta had asked Harry to have lunch with her at the onsite café. She was slightly subtler in her probing than her husband, but her intent was the same—to protect Molly and Amelia from anyone who might hurt them.

Harry badly wanted to prove himself to Greta, but

all he could do was answer her questions openly and honestly...even when his answers didn't necessarily reflect well on him. Particularly when he admitted that he'd been the one to end his relationship with Molly all those years ago.

The ferry home was crowded with both employees and visitors. Though Molly had been working hard all day, and was now officially off the clock, she was still happy to answer questions about the castle on the trip. Harry felt the same way about his work—he'd study history even if no one paid him for it.

They disembarked, then headed back to the high school to watch Amelia's first partial dress rehearsal for *The Sound of Music*. Amelia had texted them an hour ago to let them know it was open to the families of the performers and that she'd love it if they came.

"I can't wait to see her as Louisa," Harry said.

"The role is perfect for her—she's always had her nose in a book."

"Just like you."

"And you too."

When she smiled at him, Harry was relieved that he hadn't scared her away by coming on so strong inside the castle shop. She wasn't exactly throwing herself into his arms...but she wasn't shutting him out either.

From his studies of battle plans over the past decade, he knew that progress couldn't always be measured in clear wins. Often, not having to retreat was cause for celebration, because it meant you could return the next day with a better-honed strategy.

As soon as they walked into the auditorium, Amelia called them over. "Mom, Dad!" Her hair was braided and pinned up, and she was wearing a dirndl that looked like it could very well have been made out of old curtains. "Remember, this is our first dress rehearsal, so we're probably going to suck."

"No matter what you sound like," Harry replied, "I'm going to be impressed."

"You're just like Mom. I can never get an honest critique out of her, no matter how hard I try."

"I'm always honest," Molly protested. "It's just that you've been amazing in every show you've ever been in."

"Even the one where I threw up halfway through my solo?"

Molly laughed. "Okay, so that might not have been your finest moment. Even though I still think you pulled it off. Besides, hardly anyone noticed."

"*Everyone* noticed!" Amelia turned to Harry. "Tons of people in the audience ended up barfing after I did."

Molly was still laughing. "Not tons. Only one. Maybe two."

"I've got to finish getting ready with the rest of the

cast. See you after the show." And then she was gone, disappearing backstage.

"It feels like your hair just blew back, doesn't it?" Molly joked. "Did we ever have energy like that?"

"You definitely did. You'd go from back-to-back classes, to your part-time job in the dining hall, to my place where we'd study for hours…and then we'd stay up half the night making love."

She looked around to see if anyone had heard him, though no one was standing close enough. Still, she said in a low voice, "You can't keep talking like that."

On the contrary, Harry knew reminding her how good they'd been together was *exactly* what he had to do.

"Especially when I'm sure our story has been spreading like wildfire and everyone is going to be watching us." She pointed at a row already half full of parents, kids, and teachers. "Come on, let's go sit down."

She likely believed there was strength in numbers—or rather, that he wouldn't be able to keep bringing the two of them closer if they were surrounded by other people. But Harry wasn't so easily daunted. Not when he knew that becoming a part of Amelia's and Molly's lives also meant becoming a part of their community.

He introduced himself to everyone within handshake distance, falling into easy conversation with several of the parents who had spent some time in the city before moving to Alexandria Bay. Molly, however, was noticeably silent, even going so far as to pull out her phone. It was her version of a KEEP OUT sign.

Soon, the lights went down. The orchestra began the overture's familiar melody.

And Harry was spellbound.

Amelia was brilliant in her role as the book-loving Von Trapp daughter. She was sweet and funny and sang like an angel.

He didn't think that just because he was her father. From the audience's laughter and the looks on their faces, he could tell everyone agreed with him. He wanted them all to know she was his, but he couldn't exactly stand up and shout, *That's my kid!*

Thirty minutes in, the director said, "Let's take five."

The kids were just starting to walk off stage when someone yelled, "Look out!"

The performers scattered just in time to miss being hit by the wooden backdrop of a bedroom falling over and crashing into the big bed everyone had been sitting on for *My Favorite Things*. This crash set off a chain reaction, with a set piece of a mountain falling next, and then another that was supposed to be the inside of the Von Trapp family home.

"How are we going to get this fixed by opening night?" one of the stagehands wailed.

As soon as she'd made sure no one was hurt, the director turned to the audience, looking remarkably calm amidst disaster. "Anyone out there good with a hammer?" Clearly, working with hormonal teenagers all day gave high school teachers a higher threshold for trouble than most other people.

Harry didn't think twice before standing. Helping to fix the backdrops was the perfect way to get involved with Amelia's school. What's more, he actually did have good building skills. Not only had he helped his father build his home at Summer Lake, but he'd also stepped in to manage his father's construction crew several times throughout the years.

"I've never worked on the set for a musical before," Harry said, "but I'm willing to give it a shot."

"Then don't be a stranger." The director motioned for him to head up to the stage. "We need you to get working on these backdrops right away."

"Harry." Molly put a hand on his arm. "It's really nice of you to offer, but you don't have to do this."

"I *want* to do it."

Just as he'd said in the gift shop, after a lifetime of doing the things he *had* to do, he was finally doing the things he wanted to do. Getting to be a part of his daughter's musical felt like a gift.

As was the hug Amelia gave him when he got up to the stage. The greatest gift in the entire world. "Dad, you're the best!"

It didn't matter how long he and Amelia had known each other, their bond already felt strong and pure. Amazingly, she didn't seem to be holding on to anger or frustration about the past fifteen years. Instead, she had chosen to appreciate all they'd found and had to look forward to in the future.

Whereas, Harry's family had been tethered to the past for as long as he could remember. Even thirty years later, the anniversary of his mother's passing was a hard day for his father—and Harry too, who always made sure to be with his dad in an attempt to forestall another breakdown.

Now that everyone, including Harry's father, was doing so well, was it finally possible to transcend their past? To look back at their mother's life without mourning?

Several times since reconnecting with Molly, Harry had talked about wanting to make a fresh start, though he hadn't known how exactly to go about doing it. Until now, when he realized Amelia was showing him the way with every smile, every hug, every excited plan she had for them as a family.

After all these years, Harry thought he knew what family was all about. But nothing had prepared him for a love this deep. This profound. This boundless.

For all that he'd wanted to give his heart to Molly in college, the truth was that Harry hadn't been ready to love her right.

He'd needed his daughter to help him understand what love really was.

CHAPTER SIXTEEN

While Amelia and Harry stayed on to finish up at the theater, Molly headed home to collect Aldwin from doggy day care and then get something going for dinner. She was glad for a few minutes alone to unpack her wildly careening thoughts and emotions and try to make sense of them.

Aldwin seemed happy to see her again, and yet, he didn't seem to be in any rush to leave doggy day care. Not when he had made several furry friends, among them a tiny Pekingese and a mixed-breed puppy. Janet confirmed that he had settled right in with the other dogs and was probably going to be exhausted tonight after all the fun they'd had playing together and even running along the beach at lunchtime.

Aldwin stopped to sniff every plant and pole and mailbox on the way home, making the five-minute walk three times as long. As they meandered down the block, with Aldwin nearly tugging her arm off whenever he saw a squirrel, Molly marveled at the fact that Harry had done eight hours of inventory, working harder and faster than anyone else, without complaint. He'd charmed her co-workers—even Greta and Stanley, who were extremely tough customers where eligible men were concerned. And then after making friends with half the parents in the school, he was now single-handedly saving the musical. Molly had thought the director was going to swoon when Harry stood up to offer his carpentry skills.

On top of all that, from everything he'd said to Molly today, and from every indication he'd given, he seemed to want her back.

How the heck was she going to resist him?

Somehow, she needed to firm up her self-control. Needed to stop flushing and *wanting* every time he so much as smiled at her, let alone touched her.

Despite her undeniable attraction to him, Molly couldn't risk anything where Amelia was concerned. How horrible would it be for their daughter if her mother and long-lost father started dating and then broke up in the end?

But even as she thought it, she knew it was a cop-out, at least partially. Because Molly wasn't afraid of only Amelia being hurt.

She was afraid of being hurt too.

Finally back at the cottage, Aldwin plopped down on his big pillow in the corner of the living room, while Molly went to the cupboard to pull out the fixings for homemade pizza. It was good to use her hands to mix, then knead the dough. The repetitive, physical work helped ground her a little.

Half an hour later, Molly heard laughter outside, and then the front door opened. Aldwin found enough of a second wind to barrel toward Amelia and Harry, jumping to lick their faces.

As Amelia and Harry laughed, both working to keep from toppling over at the dog's enthusiastic greeting, they looked so much alike, even in their gestures, that Molly wondered how she had never seen the resemblance before.

That right there was another reason she couldn't see how she and Harry could ever make things work as a couple: How could they, when Molly would never be able to forgive herself for believing another man was Amelia's father? Regardless of what he'd said about moving forward, would Harry—and his family—ever really be able to forgive her?

"I'm *starved*," Amelia said as she dropped her backpack on the floor and went to wash her hands, Aldwin at her heels. "Did you make pizza?"

"It's almost ready to come out of the oven." Molly smiled at Harry, hoping she looked relaxed and friendly instead of skittish and off-kilter. "We usually eat it with the works, but I know you're not a fan of mushrooms, so I left them off."

"Good memory." His grin held enough warmth to make her go hot all over, despite the warnings she'd been giving herself for the past hour. "What can I help with?"

"Everything is ready to go." She brought over the salad, feeling awkward as she moved from the kitchen into the dining area, as though he could read her thoughts and know how hard she was finding it to keep her cool around him. No other man had ever affected her the way he did. And now that they shared Amelia, their bond felt even richer, deeper.

She took the pizza out of the oven, the cheese deliciously melted, the crust perfectly crunchy, the toppings fresh from the garden, including her homemade tomato sauce.

"This is the best pizza I've ever had," Harry said after he'd all but inhaled his first slice. "Did you make everything by hand?"

"I did." He had to be wondering when she'd made such a culinary transformation—the girl he'd known in college could barely boil water. "Moving into this house was the first time I ever had a kitchen of my own." At boarding school, they had never been allowed into the kitchen. "Plus, going to restaurants with a little kid in tow was hard enough that it was always easier to eat in."

"Mom says I was a nightmare when we went out

to dinner, especially when I was tired. She says I either screamed my head off or crawled under the table and didn't want her to move me if I fell asleep."

"Fun times," Molly said with a smile, before turning back to Harry. "Anyway, I figured that if I was going to be cooking, I might as well learn how to make things taste good."

"What about you, Dad?" Amelia asked. "What's your best dish?"

"Let's put it this way—when I call the Chinese place around the corner from my apartment, I don't have to tell them what I want. They just deliver the usual."

Amelia wanted to know all about what it was like to live in the city, and Molly was happy to sit and listen to them talk. Too soon, though, Amelia left to do homework in her bedroom with headphones on and Aldwin happily ensconced on the bed beside her. Harry also gave her a draft of his book, for whenever she had the time or inclination to look at it.

Molly couldn't have been happier about all the time Amelia and Harry were spending together, especially now that he had volunteered to help with the musical. More than anything, she wanted them to bond and be close with each other.

But Amelia was a teenager with her own life—friends, school, sports, and the musical meant she was very busy indeed. Which meant that Harry had plenty of time on his hands, at least until he resumed work on his book or some other project.

Molly had been dreading this time of night, when it would be just her and Harry, alone in the living room. She couldn't risk another kiss—not when she wasn't at all sure that she'd have the self-control to walk away from temptation a second time.

"I've got a paper to write for my class tomorrow night, so I'm going to head into my room now."

"I thought you normally worked at the kitchen table?"

Of course Harry knew just what a creature of habit she was, especially when she needed to concentrate. Back in college, she'd liked to work at the same desk, on the same floor of the library.

"I do, but I've learned to work pretty much anywhere over the years." Waiting for one of Amelia's soccer games to start, sitting in a doctor's office or in a coffee shop until the end of Amelia's piano lessons.

"Okay," he said. "I just wanted to make sure my being here isn't cramping your style."

"Of course not," she said, a little more enthusiastically than she needed to.

She shouldn't have let herself be affected by his slightly sad expression, or feel as though she was abandoning him. Especially when she knew it would be nearly impossible to concentrate on her paper when he was only a few feet away. But she'd always been too soft for her own good. Not just when it came to other people, but with herself too. Someone firmer and more resolute would have marched into her bedroom and simply locked the door behind her.

Anything but saying, "Actually, maybe I will work out here for a bit."

Harry's grin made her heart beat even faster. "Great. I promise I'll keep quiet so that you can concentrate."

Both of them took out their laptops, with Molly settling in at the kitchen table and Harry sitting in the armchair by the bookcase.

Of course he had to put those darned glasses on again.

Why did he have to be so sexy?

Molly had assumed she'd stare blankly at the screen the whole time, trying not to drool over the ridiculously good-looking man in her living room. One whose kisses lit up every part of her. But she was surprised to find that when she looked over her notes on the topic—soldiers returning to their families after war and the effect on both the family structure and society as a whole—she had an entirely new perspective just days after having jotted down the notes. Probably because it didn't feel too far from her own situation with Harry.

Her fingers flew across the keyboard, the ideas coming so fast she could barely keep up. By the time she looked up, more than an hour had passed. Her shoulders had grown stiff, so she reached over her head to stretch them out. And realized Harry was smiling at her.

"Looks like you were just visited by the writing fairy."

"That hasn't happened in a long time." She couldn't believe how easy the essay had been to write. She still needed to edit it, but the hard work of getting her thoughts down in a mostly coherent way was done.

"You always were my good luck charm," he said. "Maybe I'm yours now."

Now that the rush of creativity had passed, she realized how tired she was. Too tired to keep her defenses up around the charming, handsome man who could all too easily destroy the peace and happiness she'd fought so hard to achieve without him.

"Maybe," she said as she gathered up her papers. "I should get to bed now." She closed her laptop. "Good night."

"Good night." She hoped he wasn't going to tempt her even more by getting up to give her a hug, or even another kiss. Only to be irrationally disappointed when he didn't. "See you in the morning."

As she walked down the hall to her bedroom, she could feel his gaze on her. She should *not* be wondering if he liked what he saw, many years and one child later.

Looking into the bathroom mirror while brushing her teeth, she couldn't miss the lines around her eyes and mouth. Silently, she reminded herself that the handful of men she'd dated over the past few years had seemed to find her plenty attractive enough. Though it hadn't worked out with any of them—primarily, if she was being totally honest with herself, because none of them were Harry—one day she hoped to find someone who was willing to open himself up to her and let her into his life.

Ugh, she was so tired she was falling into the trap of overthinking everything. Surely, after a good night's sleep, she'd be ready to face another day with all of her defenses intact.

In any case, there was no way another kiss was going to happen tonight—no matter what, she wasn't going to risk running into him again by leaving her bedroom until morning. She and Harry were going to make it through tonight as nothing more than two friendly co-parents sleeping in separate bedrooms.

She pulled off her clothes, pulled on the silky top she liked to sleep in, then crawled under the covers. Turning off her bedside lamp, she closed her eyes, snuggling into her pillow, ready for sleep to take her.

Drip.

She scrunched her eyes shut, willing herself not to hear it.

Drop.

She gritted her teeth as she counted backward from one hundred. She'd made it to ninety-one when it came again.

Sploosh.

She sat up in bed. Gosh darn it, did the bathroom faucet really need to act up tonight, of all nights? The problem was, she'd never sleep a wink if she didn't fix it—she'd just lie there in bed waiting for the next drop of water to hit the porcelain. And of course her toolbox was in the hall closet.

Not wanting to bother getting fully dressed again, she put on a soft wrap sweater Greta had given her for Christmas. It didn't cover her completely, but it went almost to her knees, so she wasn't showing much more skin than she would have in a cocktail dress.

Molly opened her door and looked out into the hall. Harry's bedroom door was closed, and she breathed a sigh of relief. As long as she didn't wake him up, she would still be in the clear.

Two minutes later, she was back inside her room, toolbox in hand. This was the third time her faucet had started leaking, and she knew she should get a plumber in to fix it properly. But plumbers were expensive, so she'd been putting it off. Tomorrow, she'd make the call. Tonight, she simply needed to get it to stop dripping so that she could sleep.

Unfortunately, none of her usual tricks worked. Not that she had all that many plumbing tricks up her sleeve, but with a little help from DIY videos, she had always been able to take care of minor issues like this.

She yawned and reached up to cover her mouth, so exhausted she forgot she was still holding the wrench. When the heavy piece of metal clunked into her tooth, pain shot through her gums, and she dropped it.

Right on the toes of her right foot.

"Ow!"

She couldn't keep quiet as she hopped around on one foot, holding her bruised toes with her right hand, her left hand over her mouth where it was still stinging.

There was a knock at the door. "Are you okay?" Harry asked from out in the hall.

She was about to tell him that she was fine, but before she could, she did a one-legged stumble into the bathroom door frame and cried out in pain.

This time, Harry didn't wait for an invitation. Throwing open the door, he rushed inside. He'd taken off his glasses, thank God. But now he was wearing only pajama bottoms, his torso bare. He was *ridiculously* ripped, from his arms to his chest to his abdominal muscles. So gorgeous, in fact, that she had to concentrate to keep her tongue inside her sore mouth.

He'd been in good shape back in college—but surely she couldn't have forgotten *this*. What the heck kind of workouts was he doing now? And could she watch?

Heck, she could sell tickets to that show...

"Molly? Are you hurt?"

He scanned her from head to toe, which was when she realized her sweater wrap had nearly fallen completely off when she'd been jumping around her room on one foot and smashing into things.

She wasn't sure she'd ever felt more like an idiot than she did right then. She pulled the sweater back on and tied the sash tightly at her waist. "My sink was dripping, so I was trying to fix it, but I ended up dropping the wrench on my toes."

"Let me see your foot."

Before she could tell him she was fine, he was on his knees and reaching for her foot. He ran his fingers over her skin, and she shivered at his touch.

If it felt this good just to have him run his hand over her foot, how good would it feel if he caressed *all* of her? If he stopped being such a gentleman, and pulled her tight against his bare, muscular, beyond gorgeous chest?

But she already knew, didn't she? Knew precisely how her body would go up in flames, that she'd be putty in his strong, talented hands.

Molly knew better than to imagine Harry touching her...and her touching him right back. The problem was that when he was this close, she honestly didn't know how to shut these yearnings down.

"Nothing looks broken," he said, though he hadn't moved his hand from her skin yet. "Why don't you get back into bed and I'll get you some ice?"

When he left the room, she sat on her bed, pulling the sheets up so that she was fully covered, apart from her right leg and foot.

Harry came back into her bedroom holding a bag of frozen peas. "This is all I could find." He gently laid the bag over her foot. "How's that?"

Perfect, because you're here.

Thankfully, all that actually came out of her mouth was, "Perfect." Hoping he couldn't hear the slight breathlessness that had crept into her voice, she said, "I know you must be tired and want to get back to bed. But thanks for checking on me."

He looked over at the sink. "How about I take a look at the faucet?"

"I can call a plumber in the morning."

"My father might not have been around much when I was growing up," Harry said, "but he made sure we all knew our way around a toolbox. Whenever I was at his place at Summer Lake, I was helping him build or remodel something."

Just that, right there, was more than he had ever shared with her about his father back in college. In fact, hadn't Harry been pretty forthcoming about him in the store today too?

"I always wondered how your father transitioned from being a painter into construction." But she'd never had the guts to ask, not when Harry had always made it clear that talking about his father's issues was off-limits. Things were different now, though. Not only was William Amelia's grandfather, but Molly also had a feeling Harry finally *wanted* to talk to her about him. "I think I understand why he stopped painting," she said in a gentle voice, "but what made him turn to building?"

"Dad has always been good with his hands, obviously." She couldn't see Harry at the sink from her bed, but she could hear him using the wrench, or possibly a screwdriver. "I used to think that was all there was to it—that because he couldn't paint, he needed another creative outlet."

She heard the water run, then shut off, then Harry walked back into the bedroom. "Your faucet is fixed. All it needed was a new washer."

"Thank you." When they were younger, she would have let him go without pressing him for more insights about his father, but that hadn't done them any favors then, had it? "If building houses wasn't just another creative outlet for your dad, what else do you think it *was* about?"

Harry sat on the edge of the bed, his weight on the mattress making her body shift slightly in his direction.

"It's been said that my father painted hundreds of portraits of my mother because he was obsessed with her. And I'm not saying that wasn't part of it. But I also wonder if he never felt that he got it right, so he always wanted to try again. Especially when she was upset, or wasn't talking to him—that's when he would paint her the most. Almost as though he was hoping he could paint her into a different mood. Maybe even paint her into a different woman." Harry ran a hand through his hair. "I don't know if this will make any sense, but sometimes I think he was drawn to building houses because it's something that an inspector can look at every step of the way and tell him he's doing perfectly. I think it helped my father to know that he could build something that would withstand the harshest winds, the thickest snowstorms, the most thunderous rains, that would never fall or crumble. Because at least there, he got it right."

"It helped you too, didn't it?" Molly put her hand over his. "Knowing your father was able to find some peace, somewhere, at least some of the time."

Harry turned their hands over so that they were

palm to palm. "Yes, it helped."

"But what about you?" Her words were barely more than a whisper. "Where do you go when you need to find peace?"

"To my memories." Emotion thrummed through every word he spoke as he lifted their hands and brought them to his lips. "Memories of you."

CHAPTER SEVENTEEN

Harry had dreamed about Molly countless times over the years. Dreams in which they were together again, and he was stripping her bare, one piece of clothing at a time.

Only, now that they were finally together, *she* was the one stripping *him* bare, by making him want to share his emotions with her in a way he would never have let himself do before.

"Tell me you didn't forget." He pressed a kiss to the inside of her palm and felt her shiver of need. "Our laughter. Our adventures. Our passion."

"How could I?" Her words were barely more than a whisper. "You weren't just my first boyfriend. My first lover. You were my first *everything*."

"What if we tried again? Tried to get it right this time?"

"Harry…"

He was running his hands up her arms now, and though her heart was obviously torn, her body was leaning into his touch as he cupped her face.

"Tonight." He pressed a gentle kiss to her jaw. "Give me tonight." His lips found the hollow of her throat next, where her heartbeat was fluttering madly. "Give *us* tonight." He rained kisses along her neck until he reached her ear. "Let me love you the way I've wanted to love you for so long."

He nipped her earlobe, and she shuddered.

"No promises," she said. "Just one night to be to-gether again."

"No promises." But he needed her to know he wasn't just after a one-night stand. "Not yet."

She stiffened slightly, but she didn't pull away. Still, he knew he'd pushed as hard as he could tonight. Knew that she would have to make the next move, to decide whether they would keep fighting the intense desire they felt for each other...or let themselves enjoy every sizzling, hot second of it.

She gazed into his eyes, looking so deeply he won-dered if she could see all the way into the most secret parts of his soul. Then, finally, she wrapped her arms around his neck.

And kissed him.

Joy—and full-blown lust—exploded through Harry.

He wanted to be gentle, wanted to go slowly, wanted to linger and savor. But the need to have her in his arms again made it impossible to do anything but pull her against him, over him, so that they were chest to chest, hip to hip.

She laughed softly as she sprawled out on top of him, a husky sound he hadn't been sure he'd ever be lucky enough to hear again. Though it clearly hadn't been easy for her to make the decision to be with him tonight, now that she had, her laughter told him that she wasn't going to hold back.

Which was a very good thing, because Harry *definitely* wasn't planning to hold back.

Not when he was ready to make all of his wildest dreams—and hers—come true.

"You feel so good." Her voice was still soft, but as she rubbed herself over him, a sound like a purr came from her throat. She ran her hands over his bare chest, and he couldn't stop himself from flexing a little bit to make his muscles pop beneath her fingertips. "You've only gotten better with age."

He pushed the sweater off her shoulders, revealing the thin straps of the top she'd worn to bed, making sure to keep his voice for only the two of them. "So have you."

"Thank you for lying."

"I'm taking that as a challenge." He shoved the sweater all the way off, then cupped her hips with his hands. Barely covered by a pair of panties, he could feel the heat of her skin as he rolled her beneath him and drew her even closer.

"A challenge? For what?"

"To show you how incredibly beautiful you are." He slid one finger beneath the strap of her top. "Let's start here." Slowly, he slid it off her shoulder. "Your skin is so smooth." Then down lower so that the upper swell of her breast was bared to his caressing fingertips. "So soft." He used his tongue to follow the same path as his hands.

"*Harry.*"

It had been so long—far, far too long—since he'd heard her say his name like that. As though he alone held the keys to wonder, to bliss, to ultimate pleasure.

He drew down the strap on the other side, baring the swell of her other breast.

Every touch, every taste, only made him greedy for more, and though he'd intended to tease, he needed to see, to feel all of her. A moment later, he'd pulled her top all the way down, letting it pool at her waist, while he gazed raptly at her beautiful bare breasts.

"Molly." He reached for her, cupping the soft flesh in his hands, running his thumbs over the taut peaks. "I want to be gentle, but I don't know if I can be tonight. Not when I want you this much."

"Don't hold back." She threaded her hands into his hair as he lowered his mouth to her breasts. "Please, Harry. Just love me."

He didn't know if she realized what she'd just

said—that she'd asked him to *love* her. But as he drew circles over her aroused skin with his tongue, he could focus only on how much he wanted her. How nothing had ever been this good, not even when they were in college. How he'd never get enough of hearing her breathy sounds of pleasure as he moved from one breast to the other, of feeling her arch into him and knowing how badly she wanted to get even closer to him, because that was exactly what he wanted from her.

Years of longing, of waking up from dreaming of her and wishing it was real, made his hands, his movements, a little shaky as he reached for her panties and yanked them, along with the fabric around her waist, down her legs.

He shifted so that he could take all of her in, head to toe. "So damned beautiful." He had to touch, had to stroke, had to worship. Both of them watched, breath held, as he ran his hand from her breasts, over her stomach, then down between her thighs.

As soon as he touched her—so hot, so slick, so ready—a low moan escaped her lips and her eyelids fluttered shut. She arched her hips into his hand, and he captured her mouth in a searing kiss.

His tongue danced with hers as she writhed beneath him, so beautifully responsive she took his breath away.

"Nothing has ever been this good." He needed her to know the truth. *His* truth. Just as he needed her to know how much he valued her, every part of her. "Give me your pleasure, Molly. Come apart for me so that I can take you right back up to the peak, again and again. Let me love you tonight the way you deserve to be loved."

With every word he spoke, her hips quickened against his hand, her skin growing slicker, more aroused...until the moment a gasp left her lips and she pulled him to her, shuddering as he closed his mouth over hers and drank in her cries of pleasure.

At last, she stilled. Soft, and warm, and well loved.

Though a part of him wanted to keep holding her close, to stroke her hair, to breathe her in and relish the feel of her heart pounding against his, there was so much more he had to know. Would she still go crazy when he put his mouth over her the way she used to? So crazy that he'd barely have time to move, to think, before she wrapped her legs around him to take him straight to heaven with her?

He lingered at her lips a few seconds longer, then began the slow, sweet trip with his mouth over her neck, her shoulders, the hollow of her collarbone, her gorgeous breasts, the aroused peaks tempting him to savor them, before continuing down over her stomach to the sweetest part of her.

All the while, she was running her hands over his arms, his shoulders, his back. Any part of him she could reach. Instead of being replete, sated, if anything her touch had grown more feverish after her first climax.

"Do you remember the first time we were together?" He murmured the words against the lowest part of her belly. "When you were so innocent...and I was desperate to take you to the other side? Do you remember how you didn't know if you should let me taste you like this—" He licked her and her hips lifted.

"But then after you did," she whispered, "I didn't want you to ever stop."

Though hearing her say how much she'd loved being with him didn't erase the darkness from their past, it did help draw more light to the surface. Enough light that he hoped one day it would be all they could see. All they would remember when they looked back.

He took another taste of her, longer this time, relishing the chance to give both of them such fierce pleasure. "And now?" He was almost beyond words, nearly beyond thought. "Do you want me to stop?"

"No." She gasped the word as he put his hands on her thighs to spread her wider, hooked her legs over his shoulders, then reached for her hands to hold her tight. *"Never stop."*

Right then, right there, Harry nearly lost it. With Molly's hands gripping his. With her hips bucking against his mouth in an uneven rhythm. With her taste on his tongue. With her heat all around him.

Somehow, he held on to his control. Because he knew that if he could just make it through the most gorgeous orgasm that he'd ever been blessed to experience, amazingly, there would be more.

More.

My God, it was unthinkable that there could be more than this.

And yet...

Even with tremors still racking her frame, she was already moving. Already using her hands on his shoulders to pull him up and over to his back. Already climbing up over him. Already threading her hands into his hair and kissing him with enough passion to steal what was left of his breath away. Already shifting her hips over his so that she could take him inside with just the slightest movement.

She was nearly there—and so was he—when he realized, "I don't have any protection."

For all that he'd wished for the chance to be with her again, he'd never thought it would happen tonight. And even if he had, he would never have presumed to bring both frozen peas *and* condoms into her bedroom.

"I'm clean." She didn't move away. The opposite, in fact, her heat searing him as he throbbed against her. So desperate to be one with her again that he had no idea how he was managing to keep his hips still. "And I can't get pregnant. Not this week."

"There hasn't been anyone for a long time," he told her as he cupped her face to bring her mouth back to his. "And never without protection." But that wasn't good enough. "There's never been anyone like you, Molly. There never will be. Only you."

Before he could say anything more, she rocked her hips and took him inside in a glorious rush of mind-blowing pleasure. Nothing else mattered but moving with her, under her, inside of her.

Threading their fingers together, she lifted herself up on her knees so that she could take him more deeply with every thrust of her hips. He took her, gave to her, loved her with every ounce of who he was, body and soul.

Looking into her eyes, he knew he would never take her for granted ever again. No matter what else was going on in his life, Molly, and the beautiful family they made together, would always come first, always be the center of his heart.

And when she pressed her lips to his, the sweet emotion behind her kiss was what finally drove their bodies over the edge into ecstasy.

For long minutes, Harry couldn't hear anything beyond the pounding of his heartbeat in his ears, couldn't feel anything but the aftershocks of the fiercest pleasure imaginable. They lay curled together on her bed, sweat drying on their skin as they both worked to catch their breath.

After a while, he realized that she'd fallen asleep. In the circle of his arms, right where he wanted her to be from this moment forward.

His chest swelled at the sure knowledge that she would have let herself sleep only if she felt safe. For all the mistakes he'd made in the past, he hoped this meant he was finally getting at least a few things right.

Moving carefully so that he didn't wake her, he pulled the covers up over them, pressed a kiss to the top of her head, then whispered, "I love you," before closing his eyes and letting sleep take him too.

CHAPTER EIGHTEEN

The sun was barely rising when Molly's eyelids fluttered open. Still half asleep, she smiled as she thought about the wonderful dream she'd had, one in which all of her forbidden fantasies had come to life.

The shift of an arm over her waist—a very muscular arm—brought her completely awake.

How could she have thought it was a dream, even for five seconds?

And how could she have thought this was okay? That she and Harry could have one night together, one night to experience again the headiest pleasure she'd ever known, without ramifications?

It was an understatement to say that things with Harry had already been complicated. She'd known better than to further complicate them with sex.

Especially when it felt like so much *more* than sex.

The last thing she should do was let herself fall for Harry *again*. But if ever there was a fast train to falling for him, it was this. This warmth. This connection. This joy. This all-encompassing pleasure.

Last night, as soon as he'd looked into her eyes...told her that memories of her were what had gotten him through all the years...put his hand over hers and pressed a kiss to her skin? It truly had felt like being tossed onto a roller coaster right before it took off at full speed, then loving every moment of the thrilling ride.

Only now, in the clear light of day, was she forced to admit what a fool she'd been. To risk everything so hard won. Her independence. Even, possibly, her relationship with her daughter, if Amelia caught wind of what had happened and wasn't okay with it.

Okay, so all the signs pointed to Amelia hoping Molly and Harry would get back together. But that didn't mean she wanted her daughter to find out about them this way.

Especially when Molly still had no idea what *them* even meant just yet.

She wriggled out of Harry's arms. "Harry." She whispered his name, but he didn't budge.

It didn't help that he always looked so sexy in the morning, with his morning stubble and his bare chest and his...

No. She couldn't allow herself to go there. Not when it would only make her want a play-by-play repeat of last night.

She already wanted that, but it didn't matter right

now. He needed to get back to his bedroom before Amelia woke up.

Molly put her hands on his shoulders and shook him, just hard enough to get his attention. "Harry, wake up!"

At last, his eyes opened. Confusion—and then unfettered joy—lit them. "Molly." He reached for her. "Come lie down with me."

She'd never wanted anything so much. Just to lay her head on his chest and listen to his heart beat while he held her. She had to force herself to say, "You need to go back to your bedroom. Now, before Amelia wakes up."

"She'll understand." He tugged her so that she was lying on top of him, skin to skin. Every inch of her heated up. *Wanted.* She was about to lose the battle with desire when he added, "We'll just explain that we're back together."

A splash of cold water shot through her veins, making her scramble off him and over to a corner of the bed. The farthest corner, with the sheets held up to cover her nakedness.

"We're not back together." She hated seeing the hurt in his eyes—pain she'd just put there. Still, she needed to remind him of what he'd said. "No promises. One night. That's what we agreed on."

"Last night wasn't just about our bodies." Gone

was the lazy pleasure, the sleepy joy. He was pure determination as he sat up in bed and faced her. "It wasn't just about pleasure. It was about *us*. About how we feel for each other."

"I knew it was a mistake." She hated that the beauty of the night they'd shared could be so easily lost, that every word from her mouth was eroding it further. "It shouldn't have happened."

"You know I don't agree. You know I think it's *exactly* what should have happened."

"Can't you see that there's too much at stake for us to blindly jump forward into a relationship? If it doesn't work out, Amelia will be crushed."

"Molly." Harry reached for her, and for all her big words, she couldn't stand the thought of pushing him away again when he threaded his fingers through hers. The sheet covering her fell away as he asked, "Why do you think it won't work out?"

All her fears, her worries, her insecurities rose up inside of her. "There's too much history between us."

Harry's eyes were so dark, so intense, that she actually shivered. "If anyone knows that even the darkest histories can have beauty in them—beauty that never goes away, but only gets richer and better—it's the two of us. We proved that last night, didn't we?"

"Last night all we proved is that we're both still attracted to each other and have no self-control." The words were out of her mouth before she could stop them. "Please, just *go*."

                              ★ ★ ★

Harry knew better than to internalize what Molly had just said as he crept from her room to his. She couldn't have responded to him the way she had last night, couldn't have asked him to love her, then fallen asleep so trustingly in his arms, if she truly believed that all there was between them was attraction.

But after being on cloud nine the night before, he also couldn't deny that it felt like he'd just crashed and hit the pavement with a painful *splat* this morning.

He'd been so sure that making love, even if they hadn't made any verbal promises to each other, would move them forward.

He turned on the faucet in the shower and let the water rush over him, the sound of the spray masking his groan at the realization that, at least as far as Molly was concerned, they'd taken a step backward.

He wanted another chance to convince her. Wanted more time to make his case without having to hop out of Molly's bed to sneak down the hall before Amelia saw him. But by the time he dressed and headed into the kitchen, Molly was gone.

She'd left a note on the kitchen table.

A—

I need to get to work early today, and since it's Tuesday, I have class tonight. If you're hungry, eat dinner without me and I'll make something for myself when I get home. Hopefully your dad can help you with whatever you need while I'm gone. I'll have my cell phone on, just in case.

Love you,
Mom

Feeling even crankier that there was no note for him, he was banging the pots and pans so loudly as he got bacon and eggs ready that he almost didn't hear Amelia say, "Good morning."

"Good morning, sweetheart." He opened his arms, and when she walked into them, he immediately felt a million times better. When Aldwin walked up, Harry scratched the top of his head.

"Are you going to come to school with me this morning to work on the sets?" She grabbed a piece of toast that had just popped up from the toaster and slathered it with butter and jam. Aldwin happily hoovered up the crumbs that fell on the floor. "Or are you going to work with Mom again?"

"She didn't invite me," he grumbled. "I'd love to walk over to the school with you, if that's okay with you." He was really happy to spend time working on something that meant so much to Amelia.

She let Aldwin out to take care of business, then said, "My friends couldn't stop talking about you all day. And then I got a bunch of texts last night while I was doing homework asking if you were available."

"Your *friends* want to know if *I'm* available?" He was horrified by the thought.

"No. I mean, the texts were from my friends. But their moms are the ones who want to know. Don't worry, I told them you're off the market."

"You did?"

"Of course." She looked at him like he was operating on only half his cylinders. "You're still in love with Mom, so how could you date anyone else?"

Harry had to sit down. Good thing the bacon and eggs were done, so he could turn off the burners and pull up a kitchen chair.

"How'd you know?"

"You're joking, right?" She let Aldwin back in, then took over where he'd left off in the kitchen, putting a plate of food in front of him, then sitting down with her own breakfast, Aldwin at her feet. "Every time you look at my mom, you get all gooey eyed." She forked up some eggs and swallowed them before adding, "And she gets the same way every time she looks at you."

At last, he felt more cheerful. "She does, doesn't

she?"

"Totally. Although I think she's still kind of freaked out by everything, so that's making it harder for her to see how perfect you guys are together." Amelia got up to grab the orange juice from the fridge and poured them each a glass. "Give her some time. She'll come around."

Harry had never thought he'd be getting relationship advice from a fifteen-year-old, let alone his fifteen-year-old daughter. Nonetheless, he knew she was right.

Molly needed time. Time to wrap her head around everything that had changed.

Time to get used to not being Amelia's only parent.

Time to forgive him for pushing her away in college, and to forgive herself for not knowing he could be her baby's father.

Time to see that she could trust him not to take her for granted again.

Time for him to woo her properly, with the kind of romance and care that she deserved.

CHAPTER NINETEEN

Molly had never been happier about spending the day in the storeroom in the basement beneath the Boldt Castle gift shop. Usually, doing inventory in the cold, windowless room was something she dreaded. Inventory was never fun or interesting, but at least the sun had been shining through the ground floor windows while she and Harry been counting items yesterday. And she'd loved talking with him, hearing about his family, simply being near him.

Her chest squeezed tight as she thought of how she and Harry had parted that morning. And now she'd just lost count of the boxes of castle-shaped alarm clocks. She began counting again, but it was impossible to concentrate.

If she'd asked him to come with her this morning, Harry would have offered to work beside her in the dark, cold storeroom. But she hadn't asked—instead, she'd been so worried about facing him over breakfast with Amelia at the table, that she'd hightailed it out of the cottage, then hopped on the first ferry to Heart

Island to hide.

Yes, he'd loved her breathless. And she couldn't deny she'd done the same to him.

But absolutely nothing else was clear right now.

Hopefully, by the time she emerged from the darkness, she'd have figured out *something*.

"Molly, are you down here?"

She nearly groaned at the sound of Greta's voice. Her friend always knew when she was upset—and wasn't shy about asking probing personal questions. "I'm doing inventory in the storeroom."

She heard footsteps coming down the stairs and then saw Greta's cheerful smile. "You're a superstar for doing this every year in such a claustrophobia-inducing space."

Molly hoped her friend couldn't see through the smile planted on her face, though it was a long shot. "Do you need some help upstairs?"

"We're fine in the store, but Joel called in sick, so Stanley is hoping you can take his place for the tour that's coming through the archives in a quarter of an hour."

"Sure, I'd be happy to."

"Great, I'll radio him to let him know." Though Greta had passed on the message, and truly did get claustrophobic inside the basement storeroom, she didn't leave. "How are things going at home?"

"Fine!" Molly chirped out the word, suddenly glad that there were no windows, otherwise Greta surely would have seen her face catch fire. "Harry is helping Amelia build some backdrops for her musical on Friday. The two of them are already getting so close."

"Good." Greta paused just long enough for Molly to dread whatever she was about to say next. "What about the two of you?"

"We're fine." She scrambled to think of a different word, something that might convince Greta that she wasn't head over heels for Harry—but her head was so full of memories of him running kisses down her naked body while she begged him never to stop, that she couldn't come up with anything better than, "He's trying really hard."

Oh God, why did she have to say *hard*?

"I know it's quite a transition for all of you. But if any three people can make it work, it's you, Amelia, and from what I saw yesterday, Harry." Greta looked at her watch. "Now, I'd better let you wipe off the cobwebs before you greet the tour group."

Fifteen minutes later, Molly was sharing her favorite stories about the castle with the visitors who had joined her in the archives. She showed them the original plans for the castle, a collection of black-and-white photographs that had been taken during construction, and then, finally, the love letters.

Stanley stepped in for the last few minutes and gave her a thumbs-up from the back of the group as she said, "I've always thought that the history of Boldt Castle is one of the most romantic true life love stories."

"Romantic?" a twentysomething woman said. "Don't you mean dark and tragic? George Boldt built this monument of love for his wife, but then she died before it was even completed."

"Yes," Molly said, "there is darkness. And loss. But I like to think that both George and Louise would be happy to know that instead of the castle being left to crumble, we have been able to preserve and celebrate the legacy of their love long after both of them are gone."

It struck her that it was nearly exactly what Harry had said to her—how even the darkest histories could have beauty in them. Beauty that never went away, but only grew richer.

The tour group left a few minutes later, but Stanley stayed behind.

"Listening to you always gives me a shot in the arm about working here. You sure know your stuff."

"Maybe about the castle. But as for the rest of my life…" She shook her head, feeling more confused than ever. "Lately, it feels like I'm doing everything wrong."

"Of course you've made mistakes. And you're going to keep making them. We all do." Stanley wasn't afraid to be blunt. Fortunately, he was also one of the kindest people she'd ever known. "But that's okay, because life is about a heck of a lot more than our mistakes. It's also about the fun we have. The risks we take. And more than anything, life is about the love we give, even if we're not sure it will last. Just like this castle. Even when there's every chance it might crumble in the future, we've got to hope that what we're doing right now to honor it will make it last."

Molly knew Stanley wasn't just talking about the castle. He was talking about her fear of falling in love again. For so long, she had tried to tell herself she was over Harry. But lying to herself hadn't changed a thing about how she felt.

Only, if love hadn't been enough the first time around, how could she trust that it would be enough now, when the stakes were even higher?

"I don't know what to do about Harry." The words spilled out. Stanley was so much more than a boss. He'd long ago become the father she'd never really had. "Not about his being Amelia's father—he's already a wonderful dad—but about my feelings for him."

"Have you told him you're confused?"

"No." Instead, she'd banished Harry from her bedroom this morning without letting the two of them talk things through. "At least when I was eighteen, I could chalk up my mistakes to being a kid." She sighed. "Turns out, almost sixteen years haven't made me much wiser."

"Love makes fools of us all, Molly." Stanley followed up his words with a smile. "Good thing it's definitely worth it."

* * *

Harry hadn't broken a sweat during his PhD defense. He'd strapped on a parachute and jumped out of a plane with no problem to celebrate Alec's thirtieth birthday. He'd even managed to keep his cousin Sophie's young twins happy for an entire afternoon last year, when she'd come to New York and had been craving a few hours alone at the New York Public Library.

But sitting down to a late dinner with Molly was utterly nerve-racking.

Over and over, all day long, he had reminded himself that Amelia was certain that Molly was still in love with him. And since she knew her mother better than anyone, she couldn't be wrong, could she? Just as he knew his daughter was right when she said he needed to give Molly some space to let all the changes settle for a bit before he asked her to give her heart to him again.

Though he'd had a great time at the high school

with Amelia working on the sets for *The Sound of Music* whenever she could pop in between classes, a full day away from Molly hadn't made him feel any more patient. Just the opposite.

After he'd finished up at the high school, he bought flowers for Molly, came back to the cottage and mowed the lawn, then cooked dinner, all while searching his brain to come up with the best birthday present ever. But though Molly thanked him for the flowers, the work he'd done in the yard, and for making the tacos they were just about to dig into, he still wasn't convinced anything had changed since this morning.

Especially when they proceeded to have the most wooden conversation in history.

"Thank you for holding dinner until my class ended," she said.

"You're welcome," he replied. "How was work?"

"Good."

"Are you still doing inventory?"

"Yes, I was in the storeroom today. How was working on the musical sets?"

"Great. They're all rebuilt now. They just need some touch-up paint."

Harry couldn't blame Amelia for looking between the two of them and shaking her head at how pathetic they were. From his spot at Amelia's side, even Aldwin seemed disappointed in them.

Harry had always been good at diffusing other people's charged situations. His sister had often referred to him as a mediator, in fact. But now that it was *his* situation, every time he looked at Molly, his heart started pounding, his palms started sweating, and his brain went blank.

"We were given an open reading period in my language arts class today," Amelia said into the extremely awkward, loaded silence. "So I read the draft of your book, Dad."

"Thanks for getting to it so quickly." He was also thankful that Amelia was taking charge of the conversation. "What do you think?"

Harry had never been much affected by reviews, either good or bad. While growing up listening to strangers opine endlessly about his father's paintings, Harry had instinctively understood that whether anyone liked William Sullivan's art or not, all that mattered was how his father felt about his own work. If he'd enjoyed working on his canvases—and if they gave him joy to look at once he was done—then he'd succeeded.

But as Harry waited for Amelia's feedback, he realized he was nervous. Simply because he hated the thought of disappointing her in any way, even with his academic writing.

"The subject is really interesting," she said, "but

your draft felt kind of impersonal, so I had a hard time connecting."

Not wanting Amelia to see how deeply her comment affected him, he kept his expression impassive as he said, "Could you tell me more?"

"Sure." Amelia loaded up another soft taco from the fixings he'd put into small bowls on the table, then took a large bite before continuing. "You've portrayed each famous medieval knight like he's infallible. Like he can't imagine ever making a mistake. But these men couldn't always have been so sure of themselves. Everyone gets nervous, right? Everyone blows it sometimes—or at least feels like they did." She shrugged. "I'm just thinking that if you showed us how the knights aren't actually that different from the rest of us, then it would be easier to relate to them. They wouldn't just be random figures from history whose names and battle dates we're trying to memorize. If we knew something about them, something real, it seems like their stories would make more of an impact. Does that make sense?"

"Absolutely." It would be a big undertaking to follow her advice and change his book, but he would be a fool not to when what she'd said resonated deep in his gut. He didn't want to write a *good* book, he wanted to write a *great* one. "You're one hundred percent right. I'm going to need to dig a heck of a lot deeper into the personal lives of the historical figures I'm writing about and then use that information to better inform my analysis." He leaned over to give his brilliant daughter a hug. "If you think of anything else, don't hesitate to tell me."

"There is one more thing."

"Amelia," Molly said, "maybe you should let Harry chew on what you've already told him for a bit before saying anything more."

"But he asked for my feedback, and I haven't gotten to the most important part yet."

"Go ahead, Amelia," Harry said. "I want to hear whatever you have to say." Even if it wasn't easy to take in.

"I don't want to hurt your feelings." She suddenly looked worried.

"You won't." He smiled at her. "I promise. You can't be worse than *The New York Times Book Review*."

"Phew." She smiled back. "I just wanted to add that the thing that confused me the most about your book was that it felt like it was written by a robot. I mean, you're funny and cool, but none of that comes out. It's like you don't want to delve too deep into anything you're writing about. Like you're nervous about getting real with it." The last hunk of ground beef in her soft taco spilled out onto Amelia's hands as she took her final bite, then asked, "Does that make sense?"

When she got up to wash it off, Harry was glad she couldn't see his face as he said, "It does, thanks."

Her comments had hit too close, too hard. And not just because it was clear that his book needed loads of work. Hearing her say, *It's like you don't want to delve too deep into anything...like you're nervous about getting real*, hit much deeper than that.

"Dinner was great, Dad." Amelia took her plate over and put it in the dishwasher. "Do you guys mind if I leave the table? I've got some homework to take care of, and I thought I'd take Aldwin for a quick spin around the block before he sacks out in the bedroom with me."

Molly nodded. "Sure, that's fine, honey."

Somehow, Harry managed a smile. "No problem, sweetheart. See you in the morning."

Amelia grabbed Aldwin's leash and headed out with the very happy dog.

Molly wiped her hands. "Dinner was great, Harry."

Though he hadn't finished his meal, he got up to start clearing the plates. Food was the last thing on his mind.

Molly stopped him with a hand on his arm. "What do you say we leave the mess for now and take a bottle of wine out into the backyard? It's a beautiful night."

Without waiting for his response—which was a good thing, given what a difficult time his brain was having trying to unscramble his thoughts and emotions—she grabbed two glasses, the bottle, and the opener, then headed out back.

She sat on a padded wooden bench surrounded by lavender plants, and as there were no other seats nearby, he assumed she must want him to sit beside her.

"I always break the cork." She handed him the bottle and opener. "If you wouldn't mind doing the honors." He had just started turning the screw when she said, "I'm glad you've been able to spend time with Amelia, even while she's at school. I know it means a lot to her to have that extra time with you."

"It means the world to me too. She really is a great person. Funny, smart, kind." He smiled at Molly. "Exactly like her mother, in fact."

Her lips turned up at the corners at his compliment. "Although I'm afraid she's a little more blunt than I would have been just now. Teenagers don't understand that they need to tone down what they're saying. You never really get used to them being a little too honest—but eventually you learn how to take their advice with a grain of salt."

"I'm glad she was honest. Because we both know she's one hundred percent right." He put the bottle and corkscrew down and turned to fully face Molly. "All day long, I've been trying to figure out how to stop getting things wrong with you, so that I can finally get them right. But until tonight, until she called me on barely breaking the surface, I didn't want to admit what the real problem is. It felt easier not to. Easier to pretend that I'm always confident, that I always have the answers, that I'm always secure—just like the knights I study." He rubbed his hand over his chest, as though it would help with the ache inside. "That's what I've always done, isn't it? Not just with work, but with us. I never wanted to let you in too deep, never wanted to risk letting things get *real*."

"I know how much Amelia means to you and how much you want to respect her opinions," Molly said gently. "But I hate to see you beat yourself up like this."

"If I'm beating myself up tonight, that's because it's long overdue. I can't take the easy way out anymore. I need to figure out *why* I do it, *why* I shut people out. Especially you. But God...it's not easy. My heart is actually beating harder right now than it does during the final minutes of a jousting tournament."

She reached for his hands. "We've both been through so many changes already. And I swear I didn't ask you to join me in the garden because I expected an apology from you. In fact, it's just the opposite. I wanted to apologize to you for the way I behaved this morning."

"*You* wanted to apologize to *me*?" Harry was sure he must have heard wrong.

"I shouldn't have just kicked you out of my bedroom like that."

"How could you have done anything else?"

She blinked at him. "Wait, what do you mean? What are you saying?"

"I'm saying that after everything we've been through, I was wrong to expect you to go forward into the future with me without doubts." He paused, trying to corral his thoughts into some semblance of order so that she would understand. "Almost sixteen years. That's how long I've been trying to figure out where it all went wrong. But it wasn't until dinner tonight when Amelia laid it all out for me that I think I finally understand."

He wasn't used to opening himself up like this. Not even with Molly. *Especially* not with Molly, which was why he'd lost her. But he needed to do it anyway. To finally face down his demons and push past them by not shutting down.

"When we broke up, I told myself it was the only way. That I couldn't drag you into my mess and you deserved more than I could give you. But the truth is—" A truth he'd never wanted to admit, not even to himself. "The truth is that I was afraid if I allowed any chink in my armor, the whole thing would fall apart and I would crumble to pieces. So I always thought I had to seem strong, tough, even when I was already crumbling inside."

"Oh, Harry." She moved closer and pressed their linked hands to her chest. "It couldn't have been easy for you to be everyone's white knight. I wish I could have helped carry some of the load for you."

"You already did, by being the one consistently bright thing in my life. But on that night at the lake with my father, when I wasn't able to be there with you on your birthday, when I started cracking apart, piece by piece, you finally saw the side of me that I didn't want to admit was there. That's when I knew I had to push you away, before you saw any deeper. Before you saw just how much of me was cracked and broken."

"You were never broken or cracked, Harry." Molly's words were impassioned. "You've been through so much—losing your mother, trying to help your father, helping to raise your siblings, and now finding out about Amelia. No one expects you to be strong all the time. And yet, through it all, you've always been the most brave and wonderful man I've ever known."

"You're the one who's strong. Brave. Wonderful." Harry's chest ached with everything he felt for her. "And now that you're back in my life, I don't want to let you go again. I want to do better. I *need* to do better.

Otherwise, you'll keep thinking last night was a mistake. You'll keep thinking *we're* a mistake."

At last, he realized he couldn't figure this out alone, the way he'd always tried to do. He needed Molly, and this time he wasn't going to let fear keep him from asking for her help.

"What can I do to prove to you that we're worth a second chance?"

* * *

After everything that had happened during the last few days, Molly hadn't thought anything else could surprise her. But she was absolutely floored by what Harry had just said. By how he'd opened up to her, at long last—and by how much she wanted to risk opening herself up to him too.

"Everything you just told me, the fact that you've let me see the vulnerable part of you—I can't tell you how much that means to me." She swallowed hard. "Especially because I held back too. In college, I didn't tell you how desperate I was for you to open up, to share all of yourself with me, to let me help. I'm glad I was a bright light for you then, but it wasn't enough. I should have helped you whether you asked for it or not, should have stepped in with your sister and brothers and father, even if you said you had it covered. But I was so stuck feeling like I was in last place because of my parents and how they were never there for me, that I slunk away with hurt feelings and my tail between my legs. I didn't learn true determination until later, after I had Amelia."

"You were always determined, Molly."

"Maybe in some ways. But when it came to my heart..." She hesitated. Stanley had been right—she needed to be honest with Harry, even if it might make her look and feel like a fool. "With my heart, I was just plain scared. Just like I was scared this morning when I said it was only attraction that brought us back together." With their linked hands still pressed to her chest, he must be able to feel how fast her heart was racing. "Even if it scares me, which it does, I want to be as brave as you just were and admit that it's more than that. So much more."

"Will you help me get it right this time, Molly?" he asked. "Will you give us the chance to make the three of us the family we should have been all along?"

"I think..." No, this wasn't about thinking. It was entirely about *feeling*, even though a part of her was still terrified that history would repeat itself, that she'd give her heart to Harry again, only to end up crushed and alone. "I want to be with you, Harry." He kissed her before she could continue, and the starry, breathless feeling made it nearly impossible to remember what she'd been about to say. "But we need to be honest with Amelia. I can't stand sneaking around behind her back the way we did last night. We need to tell her that we can't promise her anything, but that no matter what happens, we're both going to be there for her no matter what. Does that sound good to you?"

"Dating you again?" Harry looked happier than she'd ever seen him. "It sounds like a dream come true." He pulled her all the way into his arms and kissed her again. "But there is something you should know before we go talk with Amelia."

"What's that?" Just that quickly, her chest tightened again with the fear that lay barely below the surface.

"She's already guessed."

"She heard us last night?" Molly was horrified. Of course her daughter knew about the birds and the bees, but no one wanted to hear their parents going at it. Especially when they weren't even supposed to be a couple yet.

"I don't think so," Harry said. "But she did make a comment to me at breakfast about how it's obvious that I still love you."

Love.

Barely breathing, she asked, "Do you?"

"I do." He gazed into her eyes. "I love you, Molly. I always have. I always will."

"I…" She didn't know what to say, what to think, how to feel. She'd guessed that Amelia might want the two of them to get back together, but she hadn't thought their daughter would make such a quick leap to *love*.

He put a finger over her lips. "You don't have to say it back. Not until you're ready." He paused. "If you ever are."

Molly swallowed hard, utterly overwhelmed. But she still needed to know something. "What did she say about me?"

"That I need to give you time to wrap your head around everything." He nuzzled the nape of her neck, making her tingly all over. "Good thing I have a few ideas about making that time pass in a really, *really* fun way."

Their conversation was such a serious one that he shouldn't have been able to make her laugh. But with Harry she'd never been able to control her heart.

Even when there were no guarantees he wouldn't break it again.

CHAPTER TWENTY

Molly knocked on Amelia's half-closed bedroom door. She was lying on her stomach on her bed, doing her homework with her headphones on, while Aldwin sprawled across every last inch of available mattress space.

When Amelia looked up, Molly said in a voice loud enough to carry over the music, "Can we come in? Harry and I have something we want to talk about with you."

"Sure." Amelia pulled her earbuds out. "What's up?"

Before Molly could step inside the room, Harry reached for her hand. It felt so right—it always had—but that didn't mean she wasn't nervous about the step they were taking.

Amelia's eyes grew big when they walked into the room hand in hand. "Are you guys...?"

"Yes," Molly said. "We've agreed to start dating."

"I knew it!"

Molly was amazed by how simple Amelia made it

sound. Probably because their daughter wasn't viewing their getting back together through a lens of fear about painful history repeating itself.

Nonetheless, Molly wanted to make sure Amelia really was okay with it. She sat on the bed beside her daughter, but instead of letting go of Molly's hand, Harry pulled over the desk chair to sit on so that they could remain connected. When Molly took Amelia's hand, all three of them were linked together.

"Are you sure this is okay with you?" Molly asked.

"Why wouldn't it be?"

"Well…"

Even though she felt that she should be honest about how love didn't always work out, she couldn't bring herself to say it. Not when she so badly wanted everything to be perfect this time.

"Molly and I are going to do everything we can to get it right this time," Harry said, stepping in right when she needed him. Just the way a true partner would. "But we're not perfect, and we might screw up along the way. Especially me. Even though I promise I'm not going to stop trying to be everything your mom needs me to be."

"Just there, you're doing it again." Molly's emotions were too high for her to hold back as she turned to face Harry. "Trying to take all of the responsibility for whether our relationship works. It's up to *both* of us to make it work, up to *both* of us to keep trying even if we make some mistakes along the way."

"Are you guys already fighting?" Amelia asked.

Molly said, "Yes," at the exact moment that Harry said, "No."

The last thing Molly expected was for Amelia to laugh. "Seriously, Mom, Harry is perfect for you. Not like any of those other guys you've dated." She made a face thinking of them. "Anyway, I totally approve."

"I'm really glad to hear that," Molly said. "But if you change your mind at any point..."

"I'm not a little kid anymore," Amelia reminded them. "Half my friends' parents are divorced. And even though I don't think that would happen to you guys if you got married—'cause of the whole perfect-together thing—I could handle it. So you should do *you*, Mom." She grinned at Harry. "You too, Dad."

Molly hugged Amelia. "I love you, sweetie."

Amelia lifted her free arm for Harry. "Get in here, Dad."

Molly smiled as Harry joined the hug, saying, "You're the best, kid."

After they pulled apart, Amelia said, "All this mush-iness and hugging has made me totally lose my teenage street cred." She pretended to snarl. "Now get out."

Molly and Harry were laughing as they closed her door behind them.

"What do you say we drink that wine now?" he asked.

Molly slid her hand into Harry's. "I'd like that." She smiled up at him. "Very, very much."

★ ★ ★

An hour later, they had polished off the bottle. Molly had never been much of a drinker, but after working so hard to fight her attraction to Harry since he'd come back into her life, it was so nice to let herself be close to him that she didn't want their evening together to end. Plus, she couldn't deny that the wine helped take the edge off her worries, at least in the short term.

Frogs sang, crickets chirped, and the moon rose high in the sky as stars began to twinkle above them. The evening had grown cool, but Molly was perfectly warm with Harry's arms around her.

In the wake of their earlier intense discussion, they talked about easier things, like Harry's positive impressions of the high school and town, and Molly's funny stories about people who had visited the castle.

"Does this count as our first official date?" Molly asked.

She had shifted so that she was leaning against Harry's chest. He was running his thumb over the inside of her palm, delicious little circles of sensation that were already enough to make her insides feel molten with lust.

Harry continued to caress her skin as he said, "That depends."

She looked at him over her shoulder. "On what?"

"On whether or not I'm supposed to leave you with only a kiss good night on the first date. Because if that's the case..." He brought his hand to her cheek and stroked her lower lip, making her shiver with desire. "I'm going to blow it for sure."

"As I recall," she said in a low voice made husky with need, "our first date way back when didn't end with just a kiss good night."

"I had the best of intentions." His deep voice rumbled through her. "But I couldn't resist you." His eyes were full of heat as he said, "Just like I can't resist you now."

And then he was kissing her, and it was the sweetest, most wonderful kiss. He tasted like wine, and desire, and *Harry*.

She would never want to go back to eighteen again, not after she'd built such a great life for herself and Amelia. But as she and Harry kissed, for a few moments it was nice to feel young and sexy.

"Come to bed with me, Harry." She got up and held out her hand.

"I know I just said how much I want you, but I don't want you to think I'm expecting you to automatically share your bed with me. If you're not ready—"

"I don't know if I'll ever be ready." She would never be anything but honest with him, even if it wasn't always easy to speak the truth. "But I'm tired of using that as an excuse." She took his hands in hers and pulled him up to stand with her. "We want each other. We care about each other. But we can't predict the future. The only guarantee we're going to get is that neither of us wants to hurt the other person—and that we're both going into our new relationship with good intentions."

"Have I ever told you how beautiful your mind is?"

She smiled, going on her tippy-toes to kiss him. "Tell me again in bed."

★ ★ ★

They didn't turn any lights on, letting the moonlight streaming in through her French doors provide the illumination.

"Last night, you undressed me," she said. "Now it's my turn to undress you." She reached for his T-shirt and slowly drew it out of the waistband of his jeans. "And remember, we've got to stay really quiet so there's no chance of anyone overhearing us." She leaned forward to nip at his neck. "No matter how good it feels."

Harry's low groan sent even more heat pooling

low in her belly. As did his saying, "Just so you know, I'm already *this close* to ripping off your clothes and taking you right here on the floor."

Sweet Lord...did he have any idea how much she wanted that? For him to lose control and take her fast and hard and breathless?

Soon. She needed that to happen soon.

But first, she needed to show Harry how much she adored every single inch of him.

"Tomorrow night," she whispered, "Amelia will be sleeping over at her friend's house. Which means it will just be me and you." She ran her hands beneath his shirt, relishing the rippling muscles beneath her fingertips before she pulled up the fabric. He lifted his arms to help her get it over his head. She tossed it to the floor, then immediately leaned in to press one kiss and then another to his gorgeous bare chest. "We'll be able to do whatever we want. As loud as we want."

A low curse left his lips, one that only inflamed her more. "You're going to torture me tonight, aren't you?"

She answered him first with a smile...then by sinking to her knees.

"If you call this torture—" She undid his belt, then began to open his jeans. "—then yes, that's exactly what I'm planning."

He slid his hands into her hair. "Molly." Though

low pitched, the word was hoarse. "You don't have to do this."

"Of course I don't." She slowly pulled his zipper down, then pushed the denim to the floor. "But I *want* to do it." She cupped him through the thin fabric of his boxers. "I'm *desperate* to do it."

She felt him throb in her hand, growing bigger, harder, with every second that passed. And she was right there with him, her limbs shaky, her skin sensitive and aroused, even before she'd stripped him completely bare.

A sensual smile curved her lips as she hooked her fingers into the waistband of his boxers, then slowly drew the fabric down. Slowly enough that Harry sucked in a breath, then held it, just as she was holding hers.

It was like unwrapping the most beautiful gift. One made expressly for her pleasure.

She pressed her lips against him, and his fingers tightened in her hair, her name on his lips. But soon, her soft, sweet kisses weren't enough. She needed to run her tongue over his length again and again, until he was begging, whispered pleas that went to the very core of her. Molten heat sizzling through her from the inside out. She craved his thrusts, wanted his power, relished breaking his control, even just this little bit.

Suddenly, though, he was gone, stepping away to

kick off his socks and shoes, then lifting her into his arms. "You have no idea how much I want you to love me like that. But tonight I need all of you, Molly. I need to look into your eyes and know you're mine."

I am. I'm yours.

The words were stolen from the tip of her tongue by his kiss.

And then she was on her bed and he was stripping away her clothes, so fast that by the time his mouth covered hers again, she was naked. He rained kisses over her breasts, her stomach, her thighs, her calves. Then back up her body so that he could taste her the way she'd just tasted him. Slow, sweet licks of his tongue that made her tremble, shake, beg. And his hands most certainly weren't idle as he stroked her breasts with one, while playing over—then inside—her with the other.

She had to turn and bury her face in her pillow to muffle the sounds. But she knew she must not have been doing a very good job when Harry moved back over her and covered her mouth with his.

She wrapped her arms around his neck and her legs around his hips, kissing him with every ounce of passion inside of her at the same time that he thrust deep.

So good...

Pleasure rippled through her as they moved together, holding on so tightly to each other that she hardly knew where she ended and he began, their pleasure multiplied by the wildness of their kiss.

Lost in the beautiful sensations—Harry's strong body over hers, the gorgeous feel of him moving inside of her, losing herself to sweet abandon after so many years of self-control—for the first time, Molly held nothing back.

And she knew from his kiss, from his hands over hers—from the pure intensity that blazed from his eyes as he pulled back to look into hers and said, "I love you," just as they launched each other into total ecstasy—that he had just given her everything too.

CHAPTER TWENTY-ONE

"I've got a surprise for you."

Early Wednesday evening, Harry met Molly when the return ferry from Boldt Castle docked. Aldwin tried to leap up on her to say hello at the same time that Harry pulled her into his arms, unable to wait another second to kiss her.

Holding Harry tight with one hand, while petting Aldwin's head with the other, she said, "This is the best surprise *ever*."

He loved seeing the glow on her face from his kisses. All he wanted was to keep her happy, to see her smiling.

Okay, so that wasn't *all* he wanted.

He wanted her to say that she loved him too.

And he wanted to know that she was not only his again, but that she'd be his forever.

"There's more to your surprise." He led her over to another boat waiting in the slip not far from the ferry terminal, with Aldwin madly sniffing every speck on the ground, obviously hoping for a tasty morsel of dropped food. "Your carriage awaits."

"We're going out on this yacht tonight?" She looked as though she'd just won the lottery. "Did Amelia tell you I've always wanted to go on one of these sunset cruises?" She didn't have to tell him why she hadn't—he knew she tucked away every spare penny for Amelia's future.

That morning, once Amelia had left for school and Molly had headed for work, Harry had planned to sit down at the kitchen table with his manuscript to read through Amelia's notes. Knowing what was wrong with his book, and what he needed to do to fix it, had sparked his excitement in the project again. But first, he'd needed to make plans for tonight...and finally figure out the perfect birthday gift.

Back in college, he hadn't made Molly his priority. Everything he'd done wrong, he wanted to make right. Though he still hadn't figured out the perfect gift, he hoped this boat ride would be a start in showing Molly how much she meant to him.

"Amelia didn't mention a boat tour to me. But once, a long time ago, I asked you to take a sunset cruise with me...and then I didn't show up. I'll never make that mistake again," he vowed. "I'll never put anything before you and Amelia."

Of course, that was right when his phone rang.

Though Molly couldn't recognize the ringtone, she

guessed. "It's your father, isn't it?"

"He can wait."

"Harry, you don't have to ignore his call to prove yourself to me." She put her hand on his cheek, and it was instinct to lean into her touch. "Picking up your father's call, and making sure he's okay, doesn't make what you and I feel for each other any less."

"But what if he's calling because he needs me? What if it turns out that nothing has changed for him since college and the thought of Friday is making a wreck out of him?"

"Then you'll go and help him, with my blessing. And this time, I'll help too, however I can. So will Amelia. You're not in this alone, Harry." She gestured to the phone still buzzing in his pocket. "Go ahead and see how he is. You and I have already waited more than fifteen years for this sunset boat ride. We can wait a little longer if we have to."

Though she was speaking from the heart and wouldn't offer something she wasn't willing to give, Harry was still unsure as he pulled the phone out of his pocket and hit redial. He so badly wanted everything to be different now, with none of the hurdles in their way that had been there before, rather than right back at square one.

"Dad, it's Harry. I saw you just called."

Surprisingly, his father's reply was as cheerful and

full of energy as Harry could remember hearing. After a quick conversation, Harry was off the phone.

"Is everything okay?" Molly asked.

Harry nodded. "He was just letting me know he might be a little late to Amelia's performance on Friday night, but not to worry. He says everything is great and that he wants me to give you and Amelia his love."

"I'm glad he's doing so well."

"So am I."

"But you're still worried, aren't you?"

Harry had been a fool to think he had ever needed to keep what he was thinking or feeling from Molly, when she'd always been able to see into his heart. "It's hard not to be worried when all the evidence I have after thirty-plus years is that Friday is going to be a really hard day for him."

"Are you sure coming to Amelia's show will be okay? For all of you, not just your father. She would understand if we explained the significance of the day. You could come to a different show next year."

"I made peace with my mother's death a long time ago," Harry said. "And so have my siblings. My father is the only possible live wire."

Just then, the captain came out onto the deck. "Mr. Sullivan? Ms. Connal?" The man looked down at Aldwin, clearly not that happy to have a big dog on board, though he'd already granted permission over the phone. "Are you ready to board?"

Harry shoved his phone into his pocket. "We'd better get under way before we miss the sunset."

But Molly surprised him by reaching into his pocket and taking out his phone. "How many times do I need to say it for you to believe me? One of the things I love most about you is how close you are to your family. And until you contact Alec, Suzanne, or Drake to find out if your father really is okay or not, you're going to keep worrying about him. And I will too. So call them, or text them, or whatever else you need to do to set your mind at ease."

Despite the fact that the captain was still watching them, Harry had to kiss her.

When he finally let her go, her voice was slightly husky as she said, "Why don't I take Aldwin aboard? We can wait there while you touch base with everyone."

He appreciated the sway of her hips as she walked onto the boat, the most beautiful woman he'd ever set eyes on by far, especially when she laughed at Aldwin for turning into a big scaredy-cat once he was aboard. It was nearly enough to make Harry forget why he was still standing on the dock with his phone in his hand.

But she was right—he wouldn't feel better until he knew for sure that his father wasn't on the verge of a nervous breakdown. He sent his siblings a group text:

Harry: Dad just called. Is everything okay with him?

Alec: Think so. What did he say?

Harry: He sounded excited about something, though he didn't say what. Then said he might be late to Amelia's show on Friday, but not to worry.

Suzanne: He's fine. Don't worry about anything.

Drake: Everything is going to go great on Friday.

Harry stared at his phone, his fingers hovering over its keyboard. It seemed that his brothers and sister were working together to keep his father from losing it this year.

Had they been willing to help all along?

But he already knew the answer. Of course they had. He'd just never thought to ask them.

Harry: Whatever you guys are doing to keep him happy, thank you. I want Amelia's night, and Molly's birthday, to be perfect.

Alec: They will be.

Suzanne: We've got this, Harry. You don't need to worry.

Drake: Say hello to Amelia and Molly for us. See you Friday.

Harry grinned as he slid his phone into his pocket. Over the years, he'd heard more than one person say they wished they could have been born a Sullivan to have access to money and fame. But the true gift of being a Sullivan had nothing at all to do with fortune and spotlights.

And everything to do with family.

CHAPTER TWENTY-TWO

Molly couldn't believe Harry had chartered a yacht for the evening. She understood that he had a very successful career, but it wasn't about the money he'd spent.

No one had ever done anything so special for her. Even in college, though he might have wanted to make her feel special, their plans had always fallen through. But tonight, everything was absolutely perfect. Especially after he'd come on board grinning as he told her that his siblings had promised to make sure his father was doing okay.

Once on board, they made a video call to Amelia, who was going to spend the night at her best friend's house after final dress rehearsals at the high school theater.

Molly could tell that Harry missed Amelia already and would have wanted her to join them on their cruise if she'd been free. It warmed her heart to know that they'd been able to create such a strong bond in so short a time. She'd been so worried that the years they'd spent apart would make it difficult for them to become close. But despite the years they hadn't had together, it looked like father and daughter were going to be perfectly okay.

Molly hugged Harry tight, not wanting to let him go. Aldwin, of course, wanted to be part of the action, and when he stuck his big muzzle between them, they broke apart laughing.

Harry pulled an enormous rawhide bone from one of the bags that he must have stashed on board earlier, and once the dog was happily settled on a big pillow in the corner of the deck, Harry held out a chair for her at the dining table.

She felt as though she were living a scene from a movie, with the light breeze in her hair, the yacht moving smoothly between islands, the sun setting over the water—and the most handsome man alive sitting beside her, holding her hand. All she was missing was a fancy gown, but her jeans and the sweater he'd brought for her were keeping her perfectly warm. Not that she needed much help with that whenever Harry was around, of course...

He topped up her champagne, and she wanted to pinch herself. Was this really her life?

And could it last?

The captain had left them with a brochure that pointed out the enormous mansions on Millionaire's

Row; Tom Thumb Island, which was the smallest of the Thousand Islands; and Devil's Oven, which had been the hiding place of pirate Bill Johnston. But though they were hugely interested in history, Molly knew they'd have to do another tour one day for her to take in all the details.

Tonight, she couldn't focus on anything but how good it felt to be with Harry.

"Thank you for a wonderful evening."

"Are you enjoying yourself?"

How could he doubt it for a second? "So very much."

He kissed her, then said, "Do you remember the night we practiced waltzing at my house, and Suzanne and Drake thought it would be funny to score us?"

"Your sister kept giving us nines, and your brother wouldn't go higher than a three," she said with a laugh.

But Harry wasn't laughing. "I had planned to take you dancing, but that was another date I had to miss." Before she realized his intention, he took his phone out of his pocket, scrolled across the screen until a waltz was playing through the boat's on-board speakers, then stood up.

He reached for her hand. "Will you dance with me, Molly?"

Her heart was in her throat as she put her hand in his. The next thing she knew, he was sweeping her into his arms and around the open deck beneath the stars.

Every dream, every fantasy she'd ever had, paled beside this moment. One so wondrous she felt as though she must be sparkling like the lights reflecting on the water.

"You make me happy, Harry." No matter what happened from here on out, she needed him to know exactly how she felt this very second. "Happier than I even knew was possible."

Then she kissed him, a kiss that said everything she wasn't yet able to speak aloud. But that she hoped he heard.

And when he said, "I love you, Molly," she thought maybe he had.

* * *

They danced, and laughed, and kissed, and drank champagne until the captain let them know they were nearly back at the dock. By the time they walked back through town to her cottage—a trip that Aldwin was intent on stretching out as long as he possibly could, either by sniffing or by lifting his leg for every rock, fence post, and tree—Molly was so full of anticipation, she was almost shaking from it.

At home, Harry put Aldwin in Amelia's empty bedroom, where the dog was perfectly content to curl up into a ball on her bed and close his eyes after all the excitement of the boat ride. Harry closed the door and came back into the kitchen.

Within seconds, Molly and Harry were kissing and tearing at each other's clothes.

In their haste to get each other naked, they knocked a lamp onto the couch and stumbled into the dining table. But all that mattered was how good it felt when Harry backed her up against the wall, then put his hands on her bare hips while she wrapped her arms and legs around his waist.

With one glorious thrust, he drove into her.

All control lost, they loved each other in a frenzy of passion that stole her breath away. She'd never felt so good—so free—so utterly, wonderfully *right* as Harry's mouth came down on the arch of her neck, licking, sucking, biting in time to the movements of his hips.

It was all she could do just to hold on tight...and beg for *moremoremore*.

Fireworks exploded inside of her as he covered her mouth with his, their kiss creating a kaleidoscope of sensation beyond anything she'd ever imagined. Release shuddered through them both, rolling waves of pleasure that went on and on and on, their fierce lovemaking the absolutely perfect way to end the perfect date.

For long moments, he held her to him, their hearts pounding against each other. Eventually, she'd need to unwrap her limbs from his body and stand on her own two feet again, but Molly didn't want to put that kind of distance between them. Not yet.

Not ever.

"Don't let go," Harry said, then walked through her kitchen and down the hall with Molly still wrapped around him.

It wasn't until they were in her bathroom that he put her down. A rush of cool air threatened to chill her skin where she'd been pressed up against him, but the kiss he gave her quickly heated her back up.

He didn't let go of her hand as he leaned over and turned on the bathtub faucet. "I've been dreaming of taking a bath with you ever since I saw this tub."

Even if he hadn't been naked and touching her, his deep, rumbly voice—along with the sexy memories of the one time they'd been able to take a very naughty bath together in college—would have made her want to jump him again.

"I've been dreaming of exactly the same thing," she said.

He climbed into the water first, then held out a hand for her. He sat back in the tub, and she sank into the water with her back to his chest. Reaching for the soap, he began a very leisurely and thorough journey over her arms, her legs, her stomach. By the time he ran soap bubbles over her breasts, she was desperately aroused and full of anticipation.

Just as every taste she had of him made her want more, every climax in his arms was better than the one that came before. Already, she couldn't wait to reach that next peak.

She turned to straddle him in the tub. "I can't wait," she said, neither a plea nor an apology. But simply the truth. "I need you."

"Then take me, Molly. I'm yours."

She came down over him on a gasp, the pleasure so intense that she could barely believe she wasn't dreaming. That he was really here. In her tub. In her house. In her life.

But most of all, in her heart.

"Harry."

She looked into his eyes, and what she saw in them had pleasure streaking through her like a lightning bolt, shocking every inch of her with the power of it.

With the *joy* of it.

"I love you," he said, his words feverish against her skin. With his hands on her hips and his mouth at her breasts, he showed her yet again just how right they were together.

The perfect match in every way.

CHAPTER TWENTY-THREE

Harry and Molly took the ferry over to Heart Island together on Thursday morning. Aldwin was pleased as could be to join his friends at doggy day care again.

"Yesterday, when it was just me with him all day," Harry said as they sped across the water, "instead of being happy he got to stay home with me, I actually think he was missing his new buddies."

"Don't feel bad," Molly said. "Every kid has to fly the coop at some point."

"Do you ever think about having more? Kids, I mean, not dogs." Harry didn't want to overwhelm her, but he also didn't want to make the mistake of keeping his thoughts from her.

"Before you came back into my life, I figured one incredible daughter was more than enough to be thankful for. But now that you're here..." She shook her head. "I'm afraid my answer is going to make it sound like I'm getting ahead of myself, even though we agreed to take things slow."

At his raised eyebrow, one clearly meant to remind

her just how *not* slow they'd gone the night before, she laughed.

"Okay, maybe not slow on all fronts." He kissed her before letting her finish her thought. "You know I'm still a little gun-shy. I had so many dreams before, and when they didn't come true, I thought it was going to break me. It didn't, but the truth is that a part of me is still afraid to believe things can really be this good."

"They can." He didn't have a single doubt, not anymore. "They *are.*"

"I want to believe that."

"And if you did believe it?"

She was silent for a few moments. "Then, yes." She looked into his eyes. "I would want more children."

That was what Harry had hoped she'd say. But actually hearing it made him speechless. Mostly because he could easily see them with a baby. Or two. Heck, he would happily have enough kids with Molly to make their own soccer team.

"We're here," she said, interrupting his vivid daydream.

Molly had promised him a personal tour of the archives during her lunch break. He'd brought his laptop and manuscript pages to work on at the onsite café while she was working. He also wanted to poke around the site a bit, to see if something that would make a perfect birthday gift would jump out at him.

He hated that it had come down to the wire like this, with her birthday only one day away. He should have figured out what to give her long before now.

On the dock, Stanley helped tie up the ferry, then said hello. "It's good to see you back so soon, Harry."

"I'd like to show him the archives," Molly said. "If you don't have a tour booked for this afternoon, I was hoping we could go over there on my lunch hour."

"Why don't you go now? Kendra needed more hours to help pay off a car loan, so the store is well staffed today."

"That would be perfect, Stanley." Molly paused for a few moments. Harry couldn't quite read her expression when she looked at him, then said to her friend and boss, "Actually, would you mind coming with us? I don't want to take up too much of your time, but I wanted to talk with you about something." She turned back to Harry. "I'd like you to be there for this conversation too."

Stanley shot Harry a look over Molly's shoulder that said, *Do you know what's going on?*

Harry shook his head. Though he and Molly had shared a great deal since getting their feelings out in the open, he was currently in the dark.

The Boldt Castle archives were stunning. Surrounded by the thick stone walls, the space encapsulated a library on one side, a dozen or so display cases that held maps and plans and other historical documents relating to the castle, and a large wooden desk and leather chair.

While Harry was impressed with the parts of the castle that he'd seen so far, he could happily have moved into this room.

"Stanley," Molly said, "I was hoping we could talk about your job offer."

Harry's eyebrows went up in surprise, a mirror to Stanley's.

"As you know," she continued, "I was concerned about the longer hours and added responsibility of managing the archives. But now that Harry's here—" She smiled at him before turning back to Stanley. "—I'm ready to take on the challenge. That is, if you haven't offered the position to someone else."

"Of course I haven't!" Stanley pulled her in for a bear hug. "I'm so pleased you've agreed to take the job. You're going to be a phenomenal resource and representative for Boldt Castle."

Harry couldn't have been happier for Molly. She was the best person for the job, but that wasn't the only reason he was happy: This decision meant that she trusted him not to leave her in the lurch.

Gaining her trust was the best feeling in the world.

"Thank you," she said, beaming at Stanley's praise. "I'm really excited about it. Although I was hoping we could do a slow transition, if that's okay with you. I don't want to leave Greta or anyone else at the store feeling like I walked away without making sure they had everything they needed to proceed without me."

"You can transition however you'd like," Stanley said, "but Greta has been preparing for this day for some time now."

"She has? Even after I kept turning down the job?"

"We always held out hope that you would take it. That somehow one of our arguments would sway you. Little did we know it would take this guy showing up—" Stanley gestured to Harry with a smile. "—to seal the deal."

"You and Greta are both so good to me, and to Amelia. I don't know how I can ever repay you."

"You know you're the daughter we never had, Molly. Your happiness means the world to us. Family doesn't ever need to repay family."

Molly reached for Harry's hand. "That's exactly what Harry is always saying."

Stanley's grin grew even wider as he looked at their linked hands. "Am I right to assume that you have more than one thing to celebrate today?"

Molly's nod made Harry feel even happier. "Yes. Harry and I are making a go of it. With Amelia's blessing, of course."

"All of this good news deserves a proper celebration," Stanley said after he hugged Molly again, then gave Harry's hand a hearty pump. "I'm going to find one of those bottles of champagne we stashed away after the last donor dinner. We can all toast you and your new position as head of the archives."

As soon as he was gone, Molly took both Harry's hands in hers. "I should have talked with you about this first, since it's a decision that will impact both of us, but as soon as we stepped off the ferry, it hit me what I wanted to do. What I *needed* to do."

"You know how much I want you to take this job. And how I intend to do whatever I can to support you and Amelia as you go after your dreams." He drew her close. "I'm so proud of you for taking the leap, Molly."

He kissed her, a kiss full of all the promises he was making to her. To stay. To support. To love.

She drew back, framing his face in her hands. "Actually, this is my day to take not just one big scary leap, but two." She took a deep breath. "I love you, Harry."

Harry's breath caught. "Say it again."

"I love you. I never stopped."

He crushed his mouth to hers with a kiss that possessed at the same time that it gave. Gave *everything* he was to her.

Stanley, Greta, and a good dozen staff members were standing in the doorway when he finally let her go. "We didn't want to interrupt," Greta said with a cheeky smile. "In fact, we could come back later if that would be better."

Molly's cheeks were pink as she laughed and said, "Come in and pop the cork. I was just about to show Harry the treasures in the archives. You guys can help by showing him your favorites too."

Soon, they were all enjoying the impromptu celebration, clinking their glasses together and munching on chocolate chip cookies from a tin Greta had found in the break room. Each person showed Harry the map, or book, or piece of original molding that they found to be the most interesting.

Harry had always loved working on a college campus—the intellectual stimulation, the support from his peers, the ability to make his living by digging deep into fascinating subjects. When they were eighteen, Molly had also wanted to be a professor of history who taught and studied her subject with great passion.

The more time he spent at Boldt Castle, though, the more he realized that was exactly what she'd found here. In her own perfectly unique and brilliant way, she'd created the life for herself that she'd envisioned, without letting any hardships or struggles hold her back.

With visitors soon arriving on the island, everyone had to go back to work, leaving Harry and Molly alone.

"I'll need to leave for the store in a few minutes,"

she said, "but there's something I want to show you first." She handed him a pair of gloves, then opened a locked drawer and pulled out a fire box. She put on a pair of gloves herself before opening it. "These are George and Louise Boldt's love letters."

Harry could see the reason for Molly's reverence. The paper was faded and wrinkled, the handwriting old-fashioned, and when he picked a letter up, he swore he could actually feel the love in it.

"Aren't they amazing?"

Her voice was thick with emotion as she silently read the lines she must have read many times before, but had never made her jaded. If Harry hadn't already been head over heels in love with her, he would have fallen right then and there.

"They're absolutely beautiful, Molly. Just like you."

CHAPTER TWENTY-FOUR

The next morning, Molly woke in Harry's arms, feeling more contented than she could ever remember.

Her birthday had always been slightly bittersweet, even before things had gone so wrong with Harry, but this year there was only joy. She already felt as though she'd been given the greatest gifts in the world.

Amelia had a father who loved her.

Harry had a daughter he adored.

And Molly?

She smiled as she nestled in closer to Harry's warm, strong body. She had *everything*.

Only her lingering worries that his soon-to-arrive family would be angry with her marred what would otherwise have been perfect happiness.

"Happy birthday." Harry's lips were warm on her neck. "I love you."

She couldn't get enough of hearing it and couldn't say it enough either. "I love you too*ohhh…*"

While he kissed her neck, his hand was roaming over her naked curves. She felt insatiable, wanting to make up for so many years of lost lovemaking as quickly as possible.

Last night, they'd made love in the shower, then again in bed. Needing to be quiet only made things feel more intense as Harry captured her gasps of pleasure with his kisses, and they held on to each other so tightly, loving each other with fierce passion.

Though it had been only a matter of hours, she wanted him again. Wanted him to touch her with his big, strong, sinfully talented hands. Wanted him to make her gasp with pleasure and beg for more.

Oh yes. This was the perfect way to wake up, with Harry pressing kisses to her neck and shoulders, making her arch into him when he played over her breasts, then moaning low in her throat as he slid his hand down between her legs.

Last night, they'd teased each other. Learning every inch of each other's bodies, and pleasure, all over again. But this morning, she didn't want to wait, couldn't bear the anticipation.

Thank God, he must have felt exactly the same way, because the next thing she knew, he was gripping her hips and moving inside of her.

"Harry."

Wanting to forever remember the beauty of being so close to him, she closed her eyes and tried to memorize every moment, one glorious rush of pleasure after another in Harry's arms. But in the end, all she could do was gasp, and crave, and beg for more as they drove each other higher and higher. Until all that remained was total ecstasy.

And a love so big it took her breath away.

Her heart rate was only just beginning to return to normal when Molly rolled over to wrap herself around him, feeling blissfully happy. "That was hands down the best birthday present I've ever received."

* * *

Forty-five minutes later, it was the usual rush off to school for Amelia, who had only just emerged from the shower. Aldwin had finally forsaken his spot waiting for her outside the bathroom door to lie beneath the kitchen table instead, in hopes that bacon or eggs would soon be falling into his waiting mouth.

"Happy birthday, Mom!" Amelia gave Molly a hug. "I know I usually give you your gift at breakfast, but this year, I'm going to give it to you tonight. I don't want you to think I forgot because of the musical, or because of how excited I am about my aunts and uncles and grandpa coming to the show."

"Thanks, sweetie. I know you would never forget. And I'm excited about those things too."

Amelia picked up one of the bacon and egg sandwiches Harry had put together, breaking off a piece of bacon for Aldwin. "Thanks for making this, Dad." Her mouth was half full as she said, "I'll eat it on the way to school."

She was rushing out the door, her tennis shoes only halfway on, when she stopped. "There's a letter here." She picked up an express delivery envelope. "Looks important. There's a sticky note on it from Mrs. Bronwyn next door. She says they delivered it to her house yesterday by accident and that she's sorry she forgot to drop it by before now." Amelia jogged back inside to hand the package to Molly.

"Wait a second, honey." Molly's hands shook slightly as she held the envelope. Sensing excitement, Aldwin got up to sniff it. "I think you're going to want to see this. You too, Harry."

As he'd been loading the dishwasher, she waited until he had wiped his hands on a kitchen towel before ripping open the pull tab at the top of the envelope. "Amelia, you should do the honors."

Amelia reached inside, her face a picture of total surprise as she pulled out the piece of paper. "It's my birth certificate. With Dad's name on it!"

Molly didn't even try to keep her tears from falling as she reached for her daughter and Harry, pulling them into a hug. "This is the best birthday *ever*."

"It really is," Harry agreed.

And as Molly wiped her tears away, she saw that

she needed to wipe away his too.

* * *

"I wish Amelia could have been here to greet all of you," Molly said to Harry's siblings a few hours later out in her back garden. Aldwin, of course, was making the rounds from person to person, getting pats and begging for tasty tidbits.

Upon hearing that Harry's family was coming to Alexandria Bay to see Amelia's show, Stanley had given Molly the day off, telling her to consider it a bonus for taking the new job. This meant that she and Harry were able to put together a family picnic that afternoon.

Not wanting to hide anything from him, she'd admitted that she was nervous about seeing his siblings again. He'd tried to persuade her that they weren't holding any grudges, but she doubted they would have told Harry if they were. After all, why would they want to upset their brother when he already had so much on his plate? Even with her, they might try to hide what they felt, thinking that was what Harry wanted them to do. But she couldn't let anything fester. Not anymore.

His family had arrived in a big SUV, missing only their father, who would be arriving on his own a little later. Harry had frowned at that news, but they had assured him everything was fine.

Drake, Suzanne, and Alec had smiled as they greeted her with a hug or a handshake, saying how good it was to see her again. They'd even brought birthday presents, which was going way above and beyond.

And yet, even after she'd fetched everyone a drink and made sure they had enough food to eat, she still couldn't settle...but at the same time, she didn't quite know how to bring up her concerns.

Seizing the excuse to go inside for a new bottle of wine, she stood for a few moments at the kitchen window and watched Harry with his family. She could see how happy it made him to be with them and how much they all loved each other.

For all their troubles, she knew none of them would have traded families with anyone else. Alec, Harry, Suzanne, and Drake had always been tight-knit. And now, with the addition of their partners, they seemed closer than ever.

She couldn't help but marvel at how grown-up Suzanne and Drake were. In Molly's head, they'd forever remained high school kids, but now Suzanne was CEO of her own digital security company and Drake was a world-famous painter. She marveled yet again at how Harry and his family could all be so talented and driven, while managing to be totally unassuming about their achievements. As were their partners.

Suzanne's fiancé, Roman, was every inch the tough

bodyguard…and he was also utterly besotted with Suzanne. From what Molly had seen so far this after-noon, he knew exactly how to make her laugh and also how to make her blush like crazy.

As for Drake's fiancée, Rosa—she definitely didn't fit the profile of a self-absorbed reality TV star. If anything, she'd gone out of her way to ask Molly about her life, her career, and Amelia.

And then there were Alec and Cordelia. Truthfully, Molly still could hardly believe her eyes. Alec had been the very definition of the wild and untamed bachelor. Now, though he still had plenty of edge, he was also the most devoted husband imaginable—while his wife, who clearly felt the same way about him, constantly kept him on his toes.

"Molly?" Harry walked into the kitchen. "You okay?"

She almost nodded, but she couldn't go through with it. Because though the gathering was a whirlwind of chatter and laughter, and no one had glared or scowled at her, she still couldn't stop worrying. She and Harry had forgiven each other for the mistakes they'd made, but that didn't mean his family had.

Before this week, she would have tried to bury her fears, only to have them run rampant. She knew better now, though. Knew that facing her worries head on, and telling people how she truly felt, was the only chance she had for true, lasting relationships.

"I need to apologize to your family."

"You know I don't think that's necessary." Harry drew her close. "But I can also see that you're not going to have any sense of closure until you do."

"Thank you for supporting me." She pressed her lips to his. "Even when you think I'm wrong."

"As long as we're honest with each other, I'm pretty sure we can handle anything."

Hand in hand, they walked into the yard and sat down with everyone. "Could I say something?" Molly felt foolish and shaky, but she had to press on. "First, I want to thank all of you for making the long drive here for Amelia's show. I know how busy you all are and that you probably changed plans to be here. Amelia is on cloud nine knowing you're her family now." Molly's emotions were so close to the surface they nearly spilled over. "I am too. But I understand if you're not nearly as thrilled about me. You have every right to be angry over missing out on Amelia's life until now. I'm so sorry for hurting you. All of you. And I hope that one day you'll be able to forgive me."

"I, for one, am not mad at you." Suzanne reached out to lay her hand over Molly's. "From everything I've seen and heard, you did your best in a difficult situation—and made the same assumption about Amelia's paternity that I know I would have made in your position."

"I agree," Drake said. "And the truth is that if anyone should be apologizing, it's us."

Molly was stunned. "Why would you say that?"

"Because Dad was a mess back then." Alec answered for his siblings, speaking in his blunt way. "So
was I a lot of the time. And those two," he said as he
gestured to Suzanne and Drake, "were young enough
to still need someone to look after them. As the oldest,
I did whatever I could to help keep our family together,
but the biggest burden of all fell on Harry." He shot a
rueful glance at his brother. "Dad was beyond me. I
couldn't deal with him, could barely talk to him. I left
Harry to deal with him, and I shouldn't have."

"You don't have to apologize to me, Alec. You did
your best." Harry looked at Suzanne, then Drake. "We
all did." He turned to Molly. "And we all made mistakes. The kind of mistakes I'm not planning to make
ever again."

She leaned into him, knowing he needed her
warmth as much as she needed his. "Neither am I."

A beat later, Alec asked, "So...are we all good
now?"

Cordelia smacked her husband on the shoulder.
"That's it? That's as much of a heart-to-heart as you're
going to allow everyone to have?"

He didn't look the slightest bit chastened, especially

given the way he smacked a kiss on her lips even while her eyes flashed fire at him. But he did turn to the group and say, "If anyone else wants to lay out their heart about something, I guess now's the time."

Suzanne rolled her eyes. "If I did, I don't anymore."

That was when Molly started laughing. "You guys are the best."

"I'm assuming by *best* you mean dysfunctional screw-ups?" Drake said in a dry voice that had everyone else joining in with laughter.

"You're family," Molly said, her words serious now. "Through thick and thin. Good and bad. I always wanted Amelia to have what you do, even though it was just me. Knowing she has all of you too—it's the best feeling in the world."

"You have us too," Suzanne said. "We're going to be there for you from now on." She gave Molly a crooked grin. "Even during those times when you wish we would just get out of your business already."

"Family is all I've ever wished for." There were tears in Molly's eyes as she turned to Alec and said with a smile, "Okay, I'm good now."

Though he grinned back, his eyes looked suspiciously bright as he raised his glass in a toast. "To you and Amelia and Harry."

And as the eight of them clinked glasses, it truly was the best birthday of Molly's life, a thousand times over.

CHAPTER TWENTY-FIVE

At six thirty, after settling Aldwin on his big pillow in the corner of the living room with a chew toy Drake and Rosa had brought for him, the eight of them arrived at Amelia's school. So many phones were pulled out for pictures of them that it felt more like a movie premiere than a local high school musical.

"I'm really sorry about this," Molly said as she tried to usher them inside to their seats. "I'm afraid our little community hasn't seen this much excitement in, well, ever."

"I just hope they got my good side," Alec joked.

Rosa put her hand on Molly's shoulder. Though the rest of Harry's family was successful and well known in their fields, it was clear that Rosa was the main focus due to her notoriety from her years in reality TV. "Don't worry," she said. "We're all fine. I'm sure everyone here is really nice."

"They are," Molly said. "Once they meet you, they'll be less star struck. At least, I hope so."

Suzanne laughed. "This is nothing. You should see

what happens when our cousin Smith tries to go somewhere. It's insane. No wonder he and his wife, Valentina, honeymooned deep in the Maine woods. Our cousin Cassie has a place there."

Harry couldn't wait to introduce Amelia to the Sullivan crew in Maine, and San Francisco, and Seattle, and London—they had family pretty much everywhere, actually.

"You're here!" Amelia ran down the aisle, grinning madly.

Everyone moved in for a hug, telling her how great she looked in her costume and braids and how they couldn't wait to see her shine on stage.

"Is Grandpa here yet?" She craned her neck.

"Not yet," Harry said. "He texted and said he's about five minutes out."

Though Harry's siblings had told him everything was fine with their father, he still couldn't keep from worrying. Not after all the difficult years that had come before this one.

"Oh good," Amelia said. "I can't wait for you to guys to see our sur—" She clapped her hands over her mouth. "Actually, I've got to go backstage now. Hope you guys all love the show!"

She blew them kisses, then ran back up the aisle, all long legs, flying braids, and effervescence.

"Your daughter is the coolest," Suzanne said, then

looked at Roman. "I want one just like her."

"You took the words right out of my mouth," he replied, then kissed her.

Harry shot a look at Alec to see how he was taking the open show of affection between their sister and their friend. Amazingly, his brother seemed more relaxed about it than usual. Granted, that might be only because Cordelia was distracting him by whispering something in his ear. Among her many gifts, Alec's wife had a knack for knowing exactly when to step in with her often bullheaded husband. They really were a great fit.

Just the way Harry knew he and Molly were.

"Traffic was a nightmare!"

Harry looked up to see his father coming toward them, looking harried—but not like he was about to lose it.

"Dad." Harry and Molly both stood up. "I'd like you to meet Molly Connal."

Harry had had more than his fair share of surprises in his life. But none bigger than seeing his father give Molly a big bear hug.

"It's an honor to finally meet you." William put his hands on her shoulders and held her at arms' length. "The picture was good, but it didn't do you justice."

"It's wonderful to finally meet you too." Molly paused. "What picture would that be?"

William laughed, the sound slightly off—or maybe it just sounded that way because Harry was looking for any sign that he might fall apart.

"Just something Amelia posted," William said. "And I have to tell you, she is an absolute joy. Thank you for giving me the best granddaughter in the world. We couldn't have asked for her to have a better mother than you."

"Thank you for saying that," Molly said, obviously choked up. "And thank you for welcoming her into your family so wholeheartedly."

Were it not for the fact that hundreds of strangers were craning their necks to listen in on the conversation, Harry wouldn't have interrupted the beautiful moment. But the last thing either Molly or his father would want was to share their private drama with the entire world. Lord knew, their family had done more than enough of that over the years.

"Dad," he said, "come sit down. The show is about to start."

As the lights went down, Harry thought William smelled faintly of turpentine, which was strange considering his father rarely painted the houses he worked on with oil paint, preferring to use water based. But before he could ask his dad about it, the first strains of the overture began to sound through the auditorium.

Harry was a fan of Rodgers and Hammerstein's musicals, but he'd always found it difficult to enjoy *The Sound of Music*. It wasn't that he questioned the excellence of the music or the script. It was simply that the story was so close to his own. Too close, with a widowed father who no longer knew how to connect with his children.

As a child, though Harry had known better than to dream of a nanny appearing who would make everything better, he couldn't help but hope for the impossible. When it didn't happen, every time the movie came on TV over the years, the ache inside his chest, the knowledge that there were no magic answers to their problems, had him switching the channel.

This week, as he'd worked on the sets during Amelia's dress rehearsals, he'd been able to keep his personal feelings about the story separated from his pride in Amelia's performance. But tonight, the barriers that he'd always put up to protect himself were nowhere to be found.

Especially with his father and siblings here with him tonight.

Harry turned his gaze to his father, who was utterly rapt as Amelia sang and danced on stage. If someone had told him even one year ago that his father would be here tonight looking remarkably secure, instead of enduring one of his annual breakdowns—that *all* of them would be here together with their partners, moving happily forward rather than remaining stuck in the past...

Harry wouldn't have believed it could be possible.

Any yet, here they were. More close-knit, more connected than ever before.

He squeezed Molly's hand tightly, finally understanding just how powerful love really was.

And as he looked over at his father again, Harry couldn't help but hope that one day, love would finally be enough to heal William too.

★ ★ ★

"Amelia was amazing!"

Suzanne wasn't the only one gushing over Amelia's performance. Alec had been so impressed that he'd already sent a video clip to Smith, just in case their cousin had any female teenage roles to cast in the future.

Harry wasn't sure how he felt about his daughter being a part of Hollywood, which could be so harsh. He'd support her no matter what, of course, if that was what she wanted to do. Still, he couldn't help but hope that his and Molly's passion for history—and the careers they'd built from it—would end up being more enticing to their daughter than the lure of the spotlight.

The house lights went up for the third curtain call,

and the teens did their final bows. But just when it looked as though the audience members were about to leave their seats to congratulate the kids on their performances, the director handed the microphone to Amelia.

"Thank you again to everyone who came to our show tonight," she said, glowing from the thrill of having put on a great show. "Grandpa, are you out there?"

"I'm here," William called back.

"Come on up. It's time for our surprise."

Harry looked at Molly. *What surprise?* she mouthed, exactly echoing his own thoughts.

Strangely, however, none of his siblings seemed to be asking what was going on.

What did they know that he didn't? They'd promised to look after their father this week, but could William have fooled them into thinking he was doing better than he actually was?

"My grandpa is a really famous painter," Amelia said to the audience as Harry's father made his way up the aisle to the stage. "Some of you might have heard of him—his name is William Sullivan."

Gasps came from the crowd, and phones went up yet again as people were compelled to film more footage of the Sullivans.

"He hasn't painted anything for a long time," she

continued, "but we both wanted my mom to have an extra special birthday present this year." William walked up the steps and went to stand beside Amelia. "Do you want to say anything, Grandpa?"

He grinned at her, his voice echoing out into the audience though he didn't use the microphone. "I think you've said it all quite eloquently, thank you." Then he turned to the audience. "Happy birthday, Molly. We hope you like your gift."

Something covered in dark velvet was being wheeled out from the side of the stage. Carefully, Amelia and Harry lifted the fabric. The gasps from the people sitting around them became excited chatter.

William had painted Amelia, Molly, and Harry together.

In the back of Harry's mind, he realized the picture his father had painted must have been from the one Amelia had taken of the three of them in the kitchen that first night he'd come to stay at their cottage.

Molly gripped Harry's hand. "Did you know he was going to do this?"

"No." Harry could barely believe his eyes. "I had no idea."

No wonder William had smelled like turpentine. It wasn't because he was painting a house. It was because he was painting a canvas. His first in more than thirty years.

"He painted." Harry realized Alec, Suzanne, and Drake were all staring at him and smiling as he whispered it again. "He *painted*."

CHAPTER TWENTY-SIX

"Did you guys like the show?" Amelia was standing arm in arm with her grandfather backstage. "And what about the painting?"

"The painting is incredible, William. Thank you." Molly gave him a hug, then pulled Amelia into her arms. "And you, my love, were *amazing*."

"You really were, sweetheart." Harry hugged his daughter tight. "I've never been so proud in all my life."

"Thanks." After everyone else congratulated her, she said, "There's a big cast party at the Bonnie Castle Resort. Can you guys come?"

"We wouldn't miss it," Drake said.

Molly squeezed Harry's hand. "I'm sure your father would like some help getting the painting safely home. Why don't the rest of us go on ahead and leave you two to come to the party once you're done?"

Harry was grateful that she not only understood just how big a deal it was for his father to have done the painting, to say nothing of unveiling it in such a public way, but also that after so many years of spending this night with his father in far less happy circumstances, Harry and William needed some time alone.

"Thank you." He gently touched her cheek. "Don't think I've forgotten it's still your birthday. I promise I haven't."

She kissed him, then left with her arm around Amelia, their heads bent together as they talked and laughed.

"How about we take your painting back to the cottage?" Harry said to his father.

Together, they loaded the large frame into the back of Harry's car. The worth of any of William Sullivan's paintings was staggering, with several having been valued into the millions. But his first new painting in thirty years? A painting no one had thought would ever come to be?

The dollar figure would be astronomical. If art collectors knew it had been sitting backstage in a high school auditorium for two hours, they would lose their minds.

But for Harry, the value of his father's painting had nothing at all to do with money.

The two men drove the handful of blocks to the cottage in silence. "Why don't you get Aldwin?" Harry suggested. "We don't want him to jump on the painting. I don't think I'll have any problem carrying it into the cottage on my own."

"Don't worry, Aldwin," William said when he greeted the rambunctious dog at the front door. "I won't leave you out of the next one."

The *next* painting?

Though his father had already done the world's most unexpected thing by creating the painting in Harry's hands, he still found it hard to believe that William had truly turned a corner.

Until he and Molly decided where to hang the painting, Harry realized there was only one place he could be sure it would be safe from Aldwin's big paws and curious muzzle: on top of the dresser in the guest bedroom. The bedroom where Harry had spent only one night, because he'd spent all the rest with Molly.

Though Harry propped the painting in front of the mirror, he still saw himself staring back. And amazingly, though it should have been less accurate than real life, instead it somehow seemed more true.

His father had managed to capture the full range of Harry's feelings in the moment Amelia had taken the picture in the kitchen. Pride, happiness, hope—but also some confusion and frustration. Beside Harry, Amelia was pure light. As for how his father had portrayed Molly, with her arm slung over their daughter's shoulder and a smile on her face?

Just as she had always been, Molly was pure love.

"I never thought you'd paint again, Dad."

Harry had heard his father walk into the room, mostly because Aldwin came skidding in behind him. They'd never had this talk before, but just as he and Molly had laid everything out on the table with each other, now it was time to do the same with his father. Even if it had always felt easier *not* to talk openly about this, the truth was that none of them had benefited from that. Not at all.

After a few moments of silence, his father replied, "I didn't think I would either."

"It's Amelia, isn't it? She broke the cu—"

Harry had been about to say *curse*. But their mother's death—and their father's long decades of grief—hadn't come about because of some evil witch's spell. Lynn Sullivan had never been able to cope with her life, even before she became a wife and mother. Unfortunately, rather than seek a therapist's or doctor's help, she'd decided that it was easier to leave them all behind.

"The first time I set eyes on Amelia," his father said, "and knew that she was my granddaughter, something sparked to life inside of me. Something I hadn't felt since your mother was still alive. But that isn't the full reason why I suddenly had to paint again." William paused. "You are."

"Me?"

"Yes, and Molly too."

"But you only just met her tonight."

"I knew about her, though. Back when you were dating in college. I knew she was special to you. I knew you were in love with her. We all knew that." Suddenly, William looked bleak. "And I also know that I'm the reason you didn't stay together."

"Dad—"

"No, listen. Please. This is something I should have owned up to, and apologized for, a long time ago. I can never undo the damage I did to your life all those years ago—how every time I fell apart, I knew you would be there to put me back together, even if I tore your life to shreds as well as my own. But I hope you will accept this gift, at least. Not just the painting, but the fact that I'm taking care of myself for once. Not leaning on you, or your brothers or sister either. The anniversary of your mother's death will always be a difficult day, but I've made a promise to myself that I will make it through to tomorrow without self-pity or alcohol. From here on out, I want to celebrate the present, and the future, instead of continuing to mourn the past." His father paused, his expression raw with guilt, with anguish. "But just because I'm making these proclamations doesn't mean I expect you to forgive me. Not when I stole fifteen years from you and Molly. From

Amelia. From *everyone*."

Harry didn't think. He simply put his arms around his dad. It wasn't rare for William to break down sobbing on this day every year...but this time his breakdown had nothing to do with losing his wife.

"Tonight," Harry said, "you and Amelia proved to all of us that we don't have to do this anymore. We don't have to keep blaming ourselves, or anyone else, for what happened in the past. We don't have to feel guilty anymore. We don't have to keep hurting ourselves or each other. You're absolutely right: It's time to let go of the past, and celebrate the present, and the future." He smiled at his father. "I love you, Dad. That's all that matters, both then and now."

"I love you too, son. More than I've ever been able to show. Although I swear to you that I'm going to get better at it. I promise you that."

Both men wiped away tears, then turned back to the painting. "Your work is brilliant, Dad. Once news gets out that you're painting again—which it must be already, given how many phone cameras were flashing during its grand unveiling—you're going to be inundated with requests from galleries."

"Actually, I've already chosen a gallery for a show of new work. If I can manage to create enough work to justify a show, that is."

"I remember how much you loved working in your

studio when I was little. I have a feeling you're going to love it even more now *and* be even more prolific while you're at it." Earlier that year, his father had taken the huge step of allowing his previously unseen work to be shown at a festival in Summer Lake. But creating and showing new work was his father's fresh start—and Harry was one hundred percent confident that William Sullivan was going to prove to the world that he was an even *better* painter the second time around. "Where's the gallery located?"

"Here."

"In Alexandria Bay?" Harry couldn't have been more surprised.

"Yes. I'm going to open my own gallery. Both for my work—and to support local artists." His father was clearly relishing the fact that Harry couldn't keep his mouth from falling open at the news. "I want to focus on my family from here on out, rather than hiding away from all of you the way I have for so long. And since Amelia will be going to college in a few years, I want to spend as much time with her as I can before she leaves home. Moving here makes perfect sense. Especially as I'm sure your brothers and sister will want to have plenty of time with her too. We can still go to the lake for weekends in the summer, but if Alexandria Bay is going to be the hub for most of our family get-togethers, I don't want to miss any of them."

His father paused, looking slightly uncertain. "How does that sound to you?"

"It sounds great, Dad." Harry grinned at his father, his heart lighter than he could ever remember. "Really, really great."

* * *

Molly was having a wonderful time at Amelia's after-party. Despite how star struck the other school parents had been when they'd first seen Harry's family, as soon as they all started chatting, it was easy to see that they were just normal people. Apart from Alec's billions, and Suzanne's genius, and Drake's artistic talent, Molly thought with a smile.

Still, the evening wouldn't feel completely perfect until Harry and his father arrived to celebrate with them. Suzanne had explained to Molly how William had decided to start working on the painting the previous Sunday night, at which point Amelia had confirmed that she and her grandfather had been in cahoots over it as a special birthday surprise ever since.

Molly couldn't quite wrap her head around owning one of William Sullivan's paintings. It was like having Mick Jagger write a song for her. Or Frank Lloyd Wright building her a house to live in.

"Miss me?" Strong arms wrapped around her waist from behind.

She turned to wrap her arms around Harry's neck and press her lips to his. "Not now that you're here."

"Amelia looks happy."

She followed his gaze to the dance floor, where their daughter was tearing it up with Suzanne. Roman was standing at the edge of the space watching over them, making it perfectly clear with nothing more than his large, intimidating presence that any boys thinking of hitting on Amelia—or Suzanne—should walk away instead.

"She sure does." Molly reached up to put her hand on Harry's jaw, studying his face for a few moments. "And so do you."

"My father and I had a good talk. A *great* talk."

"Want to slip away with me for a bit to tell me about it?"

"I definitely want to slip away with you, and I'll tell you everything soon, I promise. But first, I'd like to give you your birthday present."

Taking her hand, he led her out of the crowded room and onto the wharf. It was a warm night, and with the moon shining on the water and the stars twinkling in the dark sky above, Molly felt so wonderfully happy. She didn't need Harry's birthday gift to complete her night. All she needed was Harry, holding her hand and looking at her with such love in his eyes.

"All week," he began, "I tried to figure out what to

get you for your birthday. But nothing I thought of was good enough. And nothing I could have bought for you would have meant enough."

"This has already been the most wonderful day. Between Amelia's new birth certificate, your family making peace with me, our daughter's great performance, your father surprising us with the painting, and the peace I can see in your eyes after your talk with him—I couldn't ask for anything more."

"Not even this?" He reached into the breast pocket of his jacket and pulled out an envelope.

A love letter.

Just like the ones George C. Boldt had sent to his wife.

Molly's hands trembled as she opened the envelope and slid out the paper inside.

Dear Molly,

The moment I met you, I knew you were my one true love.

For the long years that we were apart, there was never a single day when I didn't think of you. When I didn't long for you. When I didn't want to find you and beg you to give me a second chance.

All the while, you were raising our daughter, helping her grow into an incredible young woman. One brave enough to come and find her father, be-

cause you taught her how to be strong. How to take risks. How to be vulnerable against all odds—and hope that love will prevail in the end. No matter what.

Now it's my turn to be brave like Amelia, like you. I want to share every last piece of my heart with you, no matter how difficult, no matter how much safer it would feel not to take these risks. To bottle up everything I feel the way I always have before.

But if there's anyone I can risk my heart with, it's you, Molly.

It's always been you.

For so long, I used my family as an excuse to stay stuck where I was. But they were never the real reason I pulled back, never the reason I shut you out, never the reason I didn't ask you for help.

The truth is that I was scared. Scared to face my own feelings. My own grief. My own losses. As long as I focused on my family, as long as I spent all my time helping them, I never had to focus on myself.

Until you got close. So close that I knew you would want me to share my true feelings with you.

So I pushed you away. Before you could see what was really going on. Before you realized what a total mess I was.

I couldn't let you see any of that, because then I would have had to see it myself. Would have had to admit that some days—most days—my sorrow over *losing my mother, and my father too, even though he was still alive, felt like it was going to crush me.*

Somewhere in there, I started to believe my own lies: That I was the guy who always held it together no matter what. That I'd made peace with my mother's death. That I could single-handedly shoulder my father's grief. That I didn't need help taking care of my family.

But I'm not that guy, Molly.

I never was.

You knew that all along, didn't you? Knew and loved the real me, through it all.

You are the most beautiful, strong, brilliant, passionate, loving woman I've ever known. I'll never stop being thankful that somehow, some way, you fell in love with me—a man who gets it wrong nearly as often as he gets it right.

Before, I would have tried to pretend I wasn't a mess. But I don't have to pretend anymore. I know that you will always love me anyway.

Exactly the way I will always love you.

Yours forever,
Harry

By the time Molly got to the end of the letter, tears were streaming down her face. She looked up, wanting to tell Harry that she was his forever too—

When she realized he had gone down on one knee.

"Turn the letter over, Molly." His deep voice rippled over her, through her. "There's more."

P.S. Will you marry me?

P.P.S. I already asked Amelia for your hand. She said yes.

P.P.P.S. I hope you will too.

Molly sank to her knees on the planks of the wharf, put her hands on his face, and kissed him with all the love she possessed.

"Dear Harry," she began, her voice shaky, but her heart sure. "You weren't the only one who fell in love the moment we met...and who never stopped loving, even after so many years apart. And you're not the only one who was scared to be vulnerable, who used their family as an excuse not to leap, or risk, or trust. But my heart always knew best. Always knew that loving you was the best thing I could ever do. Your strength, your gentleness. Your brains, your brawn. Your laughter, your tears. Your hope, your grief. I love every single thing that makes you who you are. I'm yours forever too."

She kissed him again, then smiled before saying one more thing.

"P.S. *Yes.*"

EPILOGUE

Cassie Sullivan had thought this day would never come.

Growing up in Maine, Cassie and her six siblings had heard countless stories over the years about their Uncle William. How he'd once been one of the world's most famous painters until his wife died and he put down his brushes forever.

Standing in William's gallery in Alexandria Bay, surrounded by a dozen of his new paintings—many of his granddaughter and her big wolfhound, several of his children, plus a few Thousand Islands water-scapes—seemed like a miracle.

Cassie's father, Ethan, was standing with William. The two brothers were still catching the eyes of the women around them, even those at least thirty years younger.

All of the Sullivan men shared that same charisma, Cassie thought as a pretty redhead flirted like crazy with her brother Rory.

There were some cute guys here. Maybe she

should try some flirting and see what happened. But before she could give it any serious consideration, she looked down and realized her dress had a big chocolate smear across the front.

At the last second, she'd decided to whip up a batch of extra treats in the house she and her siblings had rented for a few days for the gallery opening. She'd been so sure she'd cleaned up.

Oh well, she thought with a shrug. She'd never be as slinky and sexy and fabulous as her cousins Lori, Sophie, Mia, and Suzanne. Or a bombshell like her sister, Lola. Or as naturally elegant as her mother, Beth. Cassie was okay with that. Really, she was. Even if every guy she dated seemed to wish she was a sexy, elegant bombshell like the other women in her family.

She supposed she shouldn't give up on her love life just yet, though. How could she, after seeing what miracles love had brought about for so many of her cousins? Especially Harry, who was the happiest man alive now that he was Amelia's proud father—and also newly engaged to her mother, Molly.

Rory walked up to her, looking rugged even in his suit. "Couldn't resist making candy hearts, could you, Cass?" He licked some dark chocolate off his fingers, and she thought she heard a couple of nearby women gasp out loud. "All our lovey-dovey cousins are really rubbing off on you, aren't they?"

"You know me. I've always been a sucker for a happy ending." Even if it wasn't her own. "More now than ever after how well everything has turned out for Uncle William."

"It's pretty cool that he started painting again. They're great paintings."

She had to laugh. Rory was a master of understatement. "It's like having Leonardo da Vinci in the family."

He nodded. "Seeing his work up close like this makes me want to be back in my studio. I'll never make anything this good, but it'd be a rush just to try."

"I know exactly how you feel." Her brother made beautiful bespoke furniture, and Cassie concocted all kinds of treats out of sugar, but their drive to create was the same regardless of the medium. "Lola has been sketching madly in her notebook all night." Their sister was a textile designer whose bold fabrics had become her signature. Clearly, creativity ran in their family's blood.

Just then, Harry clinked a spoon on his glass to get everyone's attention. "Thank you, everyone, for coming to celebrate with us on Dad's big night." He turned to smile at his father. "We're all so proud of you, Dad."

Everyone raised their glasses to toast William—not only to celebrate his magnificent paintings, but also because he had finally found peace with himself and his family.

Cassie didn't know what she would have done without her family. As long as she had them, she would always be just fine. Besides, until she could have a love story like that of her mother and father—or Harry and Molly, who had held each other's hearts for so many years against all odds—Cassie was determined to hold out for true love.

Even if it meant that the heart-shaped chocolates she made for her happy customers was as close as she was going to get to romance for the foreseeable future...

★ ★ ★ ★ ★

For news on Bella Andre's upcoming books, sign up for Bella Andre's New Release Newsletter:

BellaAndre.com/Newsletter

ABOUT THE AUTHOR

Having sold more than 7 million books, Bella Andre's novels have been #1 bestsellers around the world and have appeared on the *New York Times* and *USA Today* bestseller lists 81 times. She has been the #1 Ranked Author on a top 10 list that included Nora Roberts, JK Rowling, James Patterson and Steven King, and Publishers Weekly named Oak Press (the publishing company she created to publish her own books) the Fastest-Growing Independent Publisher in the US. After signing a groundbreaking 7-figure print-only deal with Harlequin MIRA, Bella's "The Sullivans" series has been released in paperback in the US, Canada, and Australia.

Known for "sensual, empowered stories enveloped in heady romance" (Publishers Weekly), her books have been Cosmopolitan Magazine "Red Hot Reads" twice and have been translated into ten languages. Winner of the Award of Excellence, The Washington Post called her "One of the top writers in America" and she has been featured by Entertainment Weekly, NPR, USA Today, Forbes, The Wall Street Journal, and TIME Magazine. A graduate of Stanford University, she has given keynote speeches at publishing conferences from Copenhagen to Berlin to San Francisco, including a standing-room-only keynote at Book Expo

America in New York City.

Bella also writes the *New York Times* bestselling "Four Weddings and a Fiasco" series as Lucy Kevin. Her sweet contemporary romances also include the USA Today bestselling Walker Island series written as Lucy Kevin.

If not behind her computer, you can find her reading her favorite authors, hiking, swimming or laughing. Married with two children, Bella splits her time between the Northern California wine country, a 100 year old log cabin in the Adirondacks, and a flat in London overlooking the Thames.

For a complete listing of books, as well as excerpts and contests, and to connect with Bella:

Sign up for Bella's newsletter:
BellaAndre.com/Newsletter

Visit Bella's website at:
www.BellaAndre.com

Follow Bella on Twitter at:
twitter.com/bellaandre

Join Bella on Facebook at:
facebook.com/bellaandrefans

Follow Bella on Instagram:
instagram.com/bellaandrebooks

93808777R00190

Made in the USA
Lexington, KY
18 July 2018